ISBN 978-0-9795733-0-9
Which Way: Coco and The Giz Go Green
Jeri Fink and Donna Paltrowitz
Book Web Publishing, Ltd.
www.bookwebpublishing.com

Book Cover Design by Jeremy Ryan

How To Order:
Single or bulk copies can be ordered from:
Book Web Publishing, Ltd.
PO Box 81
Bellmore, NY 11710
or online at:
www.bookwebpublishing.com

Visit us online at www.bookwebpublishing.com

Coco and The Giz Go Green

by

Jeri Fink, Donna Paltrowitz, and The Which Way Kids

Books by kids for kids

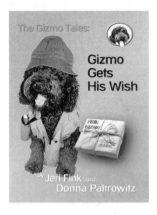

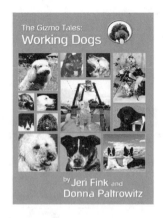

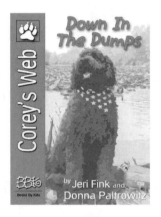

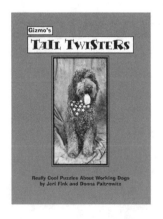

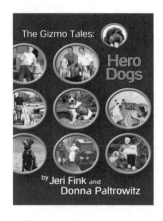

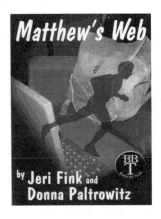

book web publishing, ltd.
p.o.b. 81, bellmore, ny 11710

Visit **www.bookwebpublishing.com**
to see how books are
written by kids for kids
and to purchase additional titles.

Special thanks from Jeri and Donna to:

Richard Fink, for his commitment to Book Web
Dr. Walter C. Woolley, who provided the original spark

Coco and The Giz for being our favorite Labradoodles
Jeremy Ryan, for his amazing artistry

Our husbands, Rick and Stuart.

For the special people dedicated to our environmental book:
Adam
Ann & Russell
Darren & Aiko
David & Shula
Meryl & Tony
Monika, Jeremy, and Edison
Shari
Stacey, Greg, and Johnny

To the special seniors in our lives, Larry Milman, Sylvia Gelernter, Harvey Fink, Robin March, and Herbert Michelson.

To the people who helped make this book a reality:
Chris Kuchta
Ellen Schwartz

and to our friends who bring us ice cream and support!
Thank you!

In loving memory of Gladys Milman, Joseph March, Ruth Roth, Judy Becker, Dora Eisenstein, Persis Burlingame, and Edna Fink.

4

We believe that kids are the best-equipped
people to talk about their lives and worlds.
Consequently, Book Web incorporates their
voices, experiences, insights, and ideas
in every book we write.
Coco and The Giz Go Green is written and
designed by kids for kids. It gives them the
unique opportunity to advocate for the earth.

Today's environmental issues
will be tomorrow's crisis. Consequently,
this book is dedicated to all the children
around the world who want to make the
earth a healthier place to live.

Jeri Fink and Donna Paltrowitz

book web publishing, ltd.
p.o.b. 81, bellmore, ny 11710
www.bookwebpublishing.com

5

Which Way
do you
go?

Warning!

This is NOT your ordinary book! Superpowers and secret signs are everywhere. Only YOU can make things happen!

Earth's superheroes, Coco and The Giz, must save the earth. They need You to control the scary paths through smog, garbage critters, and creepy crawlies. Watch out for weird cats, talking cars, and strange wizards.

Which way do you go? Choose a path full of action or a link to the real world. Read each page until you see a secret sign, then make your choice.

Secret Signs:

 means continue on to the next page.

❀ ❀ ❀ ❀ ❀ ❀ ❀ tells you to make a choice or follow a path.

 says it's the end of your path.

Coco and The Giz are on your team. Dive into fun or disaster . . . but beware, danger lurks everywhere. Keep on reading to save the earth!

Take a risk and flip to the next page

It's all
up
to
YOU!

start here

Turn to the next page ➡

YOU are alone on a dark, gloomy street. Evil noises leap from the shadows. Your heart pounds.
Something feels very wrong.
Suddenly, you're hit with a blast of fiery hot air. Bright lights flash. The air smells like burnt French fries.
You jump back, but it's too late.
A big, scary thing lands right in front of you. What is it? Why is it here?
You feel dizzy, like the whole world is spinning out of control.
A blood-curdling roar sends shivers down your back.
There's only one thing you can do.

Run!

Turn to the next page ➡

You run as fast as you can. Your breath feels like broken glass in your chest. You have never been so terrified in your life.

Without warning, a bright, green, light beam shines on your feet. Your toes freeze, sticking to the ground. You're trapped! Your heart pounds like the drums in the school band. You have no choice but to face the thing behind you. Trembling with fear, you look over your shoulder.

The thing has wheels and metal skin. Orange flames crawl along its sides. The green beam comes from something that looks like a car's headlight.

A black-tinted sunroof slides open. Two creatures jump out. One is as big as a bear; the other is small like a stuffed

animal. They're both covered in brown, curly hair and have long, shaggy beards.

"Get away from me!" You scream bravely, but they come closer and closer.

One of them roars like a lion!

"We need you!" The little creature whines.

Why would creatures like that need you? You want to run but your feet are still frozen to the ground. The hairy creatures face you.

"I'm sorry Dr. GreenWheels had to freeze your toes with the green beam," the little creature yelps. "We didn't want you to run away."

"We know all about you," the big creature woofs.

"What are you?" You ask in a shaky voice.

"We're Coco and The Giz," the little one yaps. "Our mission is to save the earth."

Coco and The Giz. They're Earth's Superheroes - dogs with a lot of crazy powers. The Giz has been a superhero for a long time. Coco, his little sister, is a superhero-in-training.

"You have to help us," Coco, the little superhero-in training whimpers. "We're going green. We need you to travel with us and write stories about our adventures."

Coco struggles to look fierce. She sticks out her chest and shows her tiny teeth. You try not to laugh.

"Why me?" you ask.

"You're famous for reporting the news as it happens," The Giz barks.

"You're the best online reporter for *Book Web News*," adds Coco.

Coco and The Giz seem to know all about you and your job. It's right in front of their noses! You carry a reporter's e-pad - a hand-held electronic notebook. You write your notes on the screen and save them like on any computer. You don't waste paper, and it all fits right into your pocket. Best of all, you can write zillions of notes and never fill it up!

Coco and The Giz probably read about how you work only on the internet - not on television or in the newspapers. You wonder if they know you like it because no one sees you. You don't have to worry about brushing your teeth or people seeing the chocolate ice cream dribbles on your tee-shirt. You don't even have to change your underwear.

"Please help us," Coco yells. It comes out more like a yawn than a superhero roar.

"I'll take the job," you grin. "Where's our first stop?"

Coco and The Giz bark happily. "First you have to meet Dr. GreenWheels."

"I already had my checkup - no doctor visits today,"

you say.

"You have to meet Dr. GreenWheels," The Giz growls.

Before you know it, The Giz puts his huge paws on your shoulders. Someone turns off the green beam. Now, you can move your feet! Slowly, your body inches forward.

The Giz pushes you, while Coco yaps like a pet monkey. Suddenly, the scary thing with the metal skin is right in your face.

"People always make such a big deal," a cranky voice says.

"Who's that?" you whisper.

"Meet Dr. GreenWheels," The Giz says. "He doesn't like people very much."

"It talks?" You hiss.

"Of course, I talk," Dr. GreenWheels grumbles. "I'm a superhero car, dummy."

Dr. GreenWheels is a very famous superhero car. He was

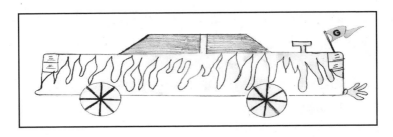

born on the island of Gizco, in the middle of the ocean. He's a very rare transformer car. Right now, he has orange flames on his metal skin. Tomorrow he might transform to look like a submarine that goes to school with purple fish at the bottom of the ocean. An hour later, he can be a rocket ship headed for an alien birthday party or a robo-rhino that hangs out at the zoo. The only way you know him is by the flag with a "G."

"Some people think the 'G' stands for GreenWheels, Green pickles, or Green slime," Coco yaks happily. "Only Dr. GreenWheels knows for sure, but he isn't telling!" She leaps on the car and licks his window.

"Ugh," Dr. GreenWheels says kindly. You can see that he really likes Coco.

The Giz shakes his head. "Act like a superhero, sis," he says to Coco.

"Get in already," Dr. GreenWheels grumbles.

Coco and The Giz jump in through the sunroof. Kids are not as lucky as dogs. You have to use the door.

Dr. GreenWheels is also a transformer inside. His dashboard is filled with buttons, lights, and screens.

Right now he smells like apple pie.

"If you push this button," Coco says, "he'll smell like pizza."

"If it will keep you quiet," Dr. GreenWheels gripes, "I'll make it smell like old sneakers."

The best thing about Dr. GreenWheels is the food. There's a green snack machine filled with organic treats. Organic foods are grown and made without chemicals. They're healthy for people, the earth, and superheroes.

"I like the turkey marshmallows," The Giz says, pressing a button on the machine. He catches the marshmallows on his long, pink tongue.

"Can I get some of Annie's Honey Bunny Grahams?" you ask. They're your favorite cookie.

"Yeah!" Coco licks your face. "You can even get Annie's Peace Pasta."

"Mmmmm!" You wipe your face. Dr. GreenWheels is really cool even if he doesn't like people. Suddenly, one of the screens starts flashing.

"That's our Earth Screen," The Giz explains. "It means that the earth needs our help."

"Let's do our job," Coco squeals, chasing her tail.

Dr. GreenWheels roars into action.

"You choose the way," The Giz barks.

Which way do you want to go?

❀ ❀ ❀ ❀ ❀ ❀ ❀

Bash Your Trash and drive to the next page ➡
Power Up and fly to page 22
Go GreenWheels and race to page 27
Hold your nose and head to Toxic Town on page 32

Dr. GreenWheels drives to a very strange place. He stops in a cloud of dust. Coco and The Giz jump out through the sunroof. You use the door because you only have two legs. Dr. GreenWheels turns off his engine and takes a nap.

Trash is everywhere. Coco and The Giz leap through it, stirring up a mess. They bark at you to catch up. You move very slowly. You have to wade through smelly old boxes, torn plastic bags from the supermarket, dented soda cans, sticky juice cartons, and lots of gooey globs.

"Where are we?" You ask.

"The landfill," Coco says.

"What's a landfill?" You want to know.

Coco whimpers. The Giz answers for her. "The garbage trucks that pick up trash bring it to places like this. We call it a garbage dump or landfill. The garbage is piled up, buried, or piled up in hills. Sometimes, garbage is burned and the ashes are brought here."

"Yeah," Coco leaps in and out of a pile of old water bottles. Green and blue labels dangle from her ears.

The Giz snarls. "Landfills are everywhere, filled with smelly garbage that can last thousands of years."

17

"Why is there so much garbage?" You ask.

The Giz pulls the old labels from Coco's ears. "People don't go green," he explains. "They make too much garbage that's bad for the earth."

"It ends up here," Coco yelps. "See?" She buries her head in a pile of chewed-up homework.

The Giz noses a stack of moldy paper. You see newspapers, magazines, empty cookie boxes, and used toilet paper. "Paper is everywhere," he adds.

"Wow!" You say, and pull out your reporter's e-pad to take notes. Suddenly, there's a deep rumbling sound.

"Something bad is happening!" Coco cries.

"Look!" The Giz points to the middle of the landfill. "The garbage is moving!"

"Let's get it," Coco leaps into the air. "I'm a superhero!"

You and The Giz look at Coco.

"What can you expect from a superhero-in-training?" The Giz chuckles.

Wade through the garbage on the next page.

You, Coco and The Giz plunge deeper into the smelly, slimy muck of the landfill. You've never been in such a disgusting place. Suddenly, a horrible monster appears in the air, right above your head.

"Stop," The Giz barks bravely.

Coco hides behind The Giz.

"One more step," the monster cries, "and I'll suck you into my slime bubble."

Now, everyone knows that superheroes don't like threats.

Coco leaps into the air and shoots her Sanitizing Breath on the monster. Since she's only a superhero-in-training, it doesn't work very well. The monster turns into a big, ugly clean monster. Then it explodes . . . into three weird characters.

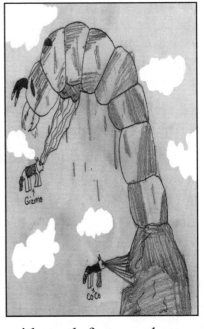

"You blew our cover!" Sheldon the cat cries. Sheldon is a super cutie cat with white puffy fur, brown spots, and blue eyes. He wears glasses with tape holding them together. On his back is a cape with math facts, and on his head is a golf hat with a goofy-looking "S" in the front.

"We're supposed to be a scary monster," Parliament Cat hisses. Her fur is black, white, and orange. Her eyes glow lime green. "Who would be scared of that?" She points to the third character.

It's a giant fuzz ball that talks as much as Coco. "I'm a clean green machine," he howls. "Now everything is messed up!"

Coco sniffs at the giant fuzz ball.

"My name is McFurry," the giant fuzz ball says, "who are you?"

"I'm Coco, a superhero-in-training," Coco replies.

"Some superhero," McFurry grumbles.

"Why did you threaten us?" The Giz asks.

"We're undercover landfill characters," Sheldon explains. We look for nasty critters that make the air and water yucky and polluted. Why are you here?"

"We're Coco and The Giz - Earth's Superheroes," The Giz woofs. "We're trying to save the earth so it doesn't become one big dump. We even brought along a reporter to tell everyone how to clean up Earth and go green."

Sheldon flicks his tail. "I'm a psychic cat," he explains. "My job is to see into the future."

"Huh?" Coco says.

"It's like this," McFurry interrupts. "Garbage makes big problems, and this dude tries to stop it, before something bad happens."

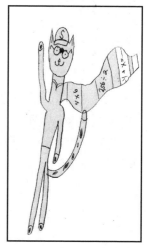

"Big deal," Parliament Cat brags. "I fly around the world on my purple skateboard to stop the garbage before it pollutes."

You look at McFurry. "What's a giant fuzz ball doing in a place like this?"

Before McFurry can answer, there's a roar behind you. It looks like a huge bone, hanging in the sky. You watch as it comes nearer. That's when you see Dr. GreenWheels' flag. Now Dr. GreenWheels looks like a hover-bone in the landfill.

"Sorry to break up this party," Dr. GreenWheels says in a grouchy voice. "There's work to be done."

Coco dives into the car.

"Let's go," she sticks her head out of the sunroof. "We have to save the world right now!"

🐾 🐾 🐾 🐾 🐾 🐾 🐾

If you want to join Sheldon, the Psychic Cat, go to page 35
If you want join Parliament Cat, fly to page 38
If you want to join McFurry, roll to page 44
If you want to dig deeper, go to page 46

Reporter's E-Pad

9 out of every 10 tons of coal is used to make electricity!

It's the most exciting night of your life!

Dr. GreenWheels transforms into bone power! Inside, he smells like ribs, right off the barbecue. The Giz licks his lips and Coco chases her tail.

"Superheroes don't chase their tails," The Giz growls.

"Only people do that," Dr. GreenWheels grumbles.

Coco yelps at The Giz. "You know it's not always easy being a superhero-in-training."

The Giz ignores her. He presses a button on the green snack-machine, filled with organic treats. Big turkey marshmallows pop out. The Giz catches them on his long pink tongue. "Take out your reporter's e-pad," The Giz says to you. "We have a great story."

Suddenly, Dr. GreenWheels lifts off the ground like a helicopter. Your heart starts to pound like crazy. You're in the air! It's really dark outside. Clouds whiz past your window. A few birds chirp angrily.

"Birds don't like superhero cars in their airspace," Coco giggles.

"We're going into hyper-speed," The Giz warns, "so we can see everything."

You don't know what that means, but it sounds good. Dr.GreenWheels makes a sharp right turn. It feels like there are a million hot dogs with gooey, yellow mustard, pressing against your chest! Dr. GreenWheels chuckles.

After a few minutes, everything slows down. You take a deep breath.

"Look," Coco yaps.

You're flying above New York City! There are lights everywhere. Times Square is filled with huge signs, flashing a zillion colors into the night. The Empire State Building is lit up in red-white-and-blue and the Statue of Liberty is in bright lights.

"Can we land on her head?" Coco yelps.

"No, Coco-nutty," Dr. GreenWheels replies gently. "It's bad for her hair."

You want to tell Coco that the Statue of Liberty doesn't have real hair, but you're afraid of making Dr. GreenWheels angry. Who knows what he does to people when he's mad?

"Full hyper-speed ahead," Coco does a doggie dance in the back seat.

"London is next," The Giz woofs.

Now it feels like a million hamburgers with green pickles pressing on your chest! Dr. GreenWheels slows down and London's Tower Bridge and Big Ben are right outside your window. They're shining in the middle of the night too!

"Let's go to Tokyo next," Coco yowls.

This time you expect the hyperspeed. You're getting used to it. You don't even think of hot dogs or hamburgers, when you see Japan with dazzling lights outside your window!

"Sydney, Australia," The Giz growls. "Tel Aviv, Israel." He continues.

You're flying around the world. The big cities are filled with bright lights, amazing moving signs, and buildings that glow in the dark.

"Awesome!" you shout.

All of a sudden the lights dim. Some places are so dark, you can't see anything. Other places are in a weak, brownish glow.

"Where are we?" you ask.

"We're flying over the houses where people live," The Giz replies.

"Where are the bright lights?" you ask.

"Reporters are supposed to use their brains, not sit on them," mumbles Dr. GreenWheels. "Figure it out!"

Turn to the next page ➤

You're not sure whether your story is about the bright lights or the dark houses.

"Lights use a lot of electricity," The Giz says.

Dr. GreenWheels makes a sharp turn. Suddenly, the smell of barbecued ribs doesn't feel that great. Your stomach does a flip-flop. You look out the window and everything is dark. Dr. GreenWheels lands in a parking lot. Only one building has lights.

"That's The Willow Pet Hotel," The Giz barks happily.

The Willow Pet Hotel looks like a lot of fun! There's music, television, and video games. Coco and The Giz leap out the sunroof. You have to use the door.

"We're checking in," Coco races ahead.

The Willow Pet Hotel is very busy inside. Cats, in cool tee-shirts, play noisy video games. A fussy poodle uses a hair dryer to fluff her pink fur. A bunch of dogs strum electric guitars and howl.

A man with a tiny beard rushes over. "Your rooms are ready," he says to Coco and The Giz. "I'm Mr. Marc," he says to you.

"What's for dinner?" The Giz asks.

"Hamburgers with deep fried kibble," Mr. Marc says. "We have beef swirl ice cream for dessert." He looks at you. "Maybe you'll try our mint bone cookies?"

You smile weakly. You have no idea why the hotel is so busy and bright, when everywhere else is so dark.

Mr. Marc reads your mind. "Lights and signs around the

world use electricity. Movie theaters and popcorn machines use electricity. Everything at home - from your rechargeable homework robot to your power soccer ball, uses electricity. We just don't have enough power to go around!"

"I've got power!" Coco fires her Amazing Tail Zap to make a mini, two-inch-high tornado."

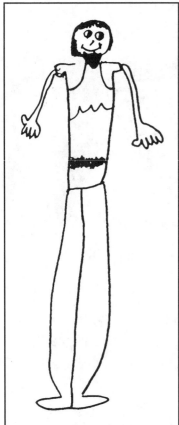

"Not that kind of power," Mr. Marc says. He waits for the tornado to blow itself out. "When we don't have enough electric power to go around," he continues, "there are blackouts and brownouts."

"Blackout steak," Coco tries to dance, but can't seem to stop spinning around and around, "is my favorite!"

"Blackouts and brownouts aren't steaks," Mr. Marc corrects her. "A blackout is when there's no electricity. A brownout is when there's less electricity," he adds. "We don't have blackouts or brownouts here at The Willow Pet Hotel."

❀ ❀ ❀ ❀ ❀ ❀ ❀

Find out why The Willow Pet Hotel has power on page 47
Dig Deeper to see the light on page 49
Forget the lights and find some people ice cream on page 48

Reporter's E-Pad

Sugar cane can be used to make a fuel for cars called ethanol. Sugar cane is the same stuff used to make jellybeans!

"Get in," Dr. GreenWheels bellows. "We can't waste any time."

Dr. GreenWheels transforms into a cool sports car. Red waves race down his metal sides. His wheels are shiny steel and his "G" flag waves in the wind.

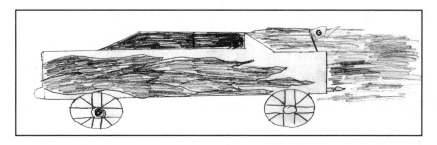

You, Coco, and The Giz jump in. Dr. GreenWheels smells like a chocolate energy bar.

"We're going to Gizco Island," Dr. GreenWheels roars.

Coco squeals and does a double flip onto the back seat.

"Easy, Coco-nutty," Dr. GreenWheels says gently.

Everyone knows about Gizco Island. It is in the middle of the ocean, named after the most popular superhero dogs -The Giz and Coco. Many superhero dogs and superhero cars are born there. Lots of dogs stay on Gizco because they love the Bone Trees in the forest, near the volcano. Strange birds and

 wild animals hide in the Kibble Bushes. The *coolest* superhero cars in the world are born on Gizco. They come from three big families - GreenWheels, HyBrids, and GasGuys.

You're really excited! It's going to be a great story for *Book Web News*. You make sure that your reporter's e-pad is ready.

"I don't like to take people to Gizco," Dr. GreenWheels grumbles.

"Why are we going there?" you ask.

"That's a dumb human question," Dr. GreenWheels says in a crabby voice.

"It's the Annual Bone Challenge," The Giz woofs, "the most amazing car race ever! They call it BYOF."

"What's that?" You ask.

"**B**ring **Y**our **O**wn **F**uel," The Giz replies. "The race lasts two days, thirty minutes, and twenty seconds. Every car has pit stops to refuel."

"Wow," you reply. "That's a lot of fuel."

"It sure is," Dr. GreenWheels rumbles. "That's the problem."

"No problem," Coco yelps. "I'll use my Amazing Tail Zap to get everyone as much fuel as they need."

"Keep your Zap under cover," The Giz advises. "You don't want to make any flat tires."

Suddenly, a green flag flashes inside the windshield. In car racing, a green flag means "go" - start the race now.

Dr. GreenWheels roars into action.

Turn to the next page ➡

Dr. GreenWheels races down the highway at hyper-speed. You whiz by trees, houses, and regular cars. Suddenly, there's a beach straight ahead. Your heart pounds. "Stop!" you cry as Dr. GreenWheels speeds over the sand and plunges into the ocean.

You close your eyes. It could be the end of your life!

"You'd think humans know that islands are surrounded by water," yells Dr. GreenWheels. "Open your eyes, dumbo - it's only water!" Slowly you open your eyes. You're still breathing. Dr. GreenWheels zips across the water . . . like a boat in hyper-speed.

Coco and The Giz laugh at you.

"You don't like cars that drive on water?" The Giz asks.

"Vrmmmmm," Dr. GreenWheels sputters. "What do you expect from people?"

After a few minutes, Coco leaps at Gizmo's tail. She pulls as hard as she can. "Look!" she yelps.

Gizco Island is right in front of you!

"We're here," Dr. GreenWheels buzzes.

Beyond the beach, there's a volcano with puffs of smoke coming from the top. Everything looks green and pretty on one side of the volcano. On the other side, it's gray.

"What's that?" you point to the gray side.

"Car emissions," The Giz snarls.

You know all about that. Car emissions are the stuff that pollutes the air when we drive. Car emissions come from using gasoline for fuel.

The Giz wrinkles his nose. "I hate the smell." He growls.

You agree. Most cars use gasoline to run. Like all fossil fuels, gas pollutes the air. Gas is very bad for the earth and people. It makes the earth sick by causing things like global warming and smog. Global warming is when the earth gets hotter and the weather changes.

"I'll make a tasty gas bubble that everyone will love," Coco cries.

"No, Coco-nutty," Dr. GreenWheels cries, but it's too late.

Coco fires her Amazing Tail Zap and a gas bubble, the size of a soccer ball, appears.

"Don't pop it!" The Giz warns, but he's too late as well.

Coco pops the bubble and bubble gum spit flies in all directions.

"You have to do your Zap homework!" The Giz barks.

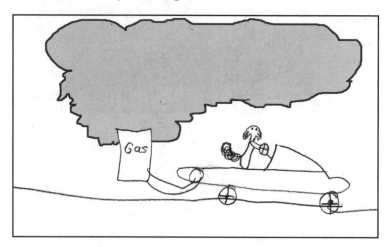

You don't say anything. You're too busy wiping bubble gum spit from your hair.

"The GasGuys live there," The Giz points to the gray side. "There's a lot of pollution because all of them use gasoline for

fuel . . . not bubble gum spit."

Looking at Coco you wonder why she didn't get bubble gum spit in her hair.

"Human kids don't like to live on that part of the island," The Giz continues. "The pollution makes them sick."

"Why is the rest of the island clear?" You ask.

"The GreenWheels use only clean fuels," Dr. GreenWheels hums. "We don't pollute the air."

"The HyBrids use a mix of gas and electricity. They're a lot better for the earth," The Giz adds.

"They're peacemakers," Dr. GreenWheels mumbles as he shifts out of hyper-speed. "The HyBrids make everyone happy."

Dr. GreenWheels docks on Gizco Island Beach.

Which way do you go?

🐾 🐾 🐾 🐾 🐾 🐾 🐾

Race with the GreenWheels on page 50
Race with the HyBrids on page 55
Race with the GasGuys on page 58
Dig Deeper on page 60

A bright light flashes on the Earth Screen. Slowly the lights form into a word: Help!

"The kids from Toxic Town are crying for help," The Giz explains. "They want to get rid of the poisons in their town."

"Cool," Coco yelps, rolling on her back and kicking her paws in the air.

"It sounds more like a garbage dump than a town," you say.

"It's the dirtiest town in the state," The Giz growls.

Dr. GreenWheels transforms into a big, clunky car covered with grease and soot. "We'll fit in," he grumbles. "It's easy to look like a pile of people junk."

The Giz reads the Earth Screen on the dashboard. "The kids in Toxic Town are in trouble," he barks. "Everything is shutting down."

With a name like Toxic Town, you're not surprised.

"We have to get there right now!" The Giz barks.

You would rather go to Annie's Homegrown and nibble on some Honey Bunny Grahams, but you're not driving. You reach into your pocket for your favorite candy. It's your last package of Jumping Chocolate Caterpillars. Dr. GreenWheels zooms into hyper speed.

Turn to the next page ➡

You arrive in Toxic Town. Everything is yucky, like a smelly dumpster that hasn't been emptied in a long time. The streets are filled with used toilet paper, piles of rotten food, and old candy wrappers. Gray clouds of smoke come from down the block. This place really needs a bath, you think.

Dr. GreenWheels stops in front of Toxic Town School.

"Get out," he commands.

You don't want to leave the car, but there's no choice. You, Coco and The Giz have to help the Toxic Town kids. You wonder what the kids look like. The three of you leave Dr. GreenWheels.

The town smells like feet. Coco and The Giz rub their noses. Your eyes water. You run into the school just to get away from the nasty air.

Toxic Town School is out of control! Kids run everywhere. Slime balls dot the walls. There's a food fight at the end of the hall. One side flings moldy orange jelly sandwiches. The other side tosses waffles with muddy butter. A bunch of little kids laugh when they slip on squashed jellybeans and banana peels. The place smells like skunk.

You want to take out your reporter's e-pad, but you're afraid it'll get too dirty!

A crowd of kids runs toward you.

A boy with mint chocolate something on his face comes forward. "My name is Bob," he says.

A girl also comes forward. "I'm Daisy," she smiles. Her white shirt is spotted with cherry candy. "We called for help."

Bob and Daisy are clearly the leaders of this group. You wonder if you would ever want to hang out with them.

A glob of chewed watermelon bubble gum hits you in the nose. "What's happening?" you ask, wiping it off.

"It's awful!" Bob and Daisy say at the same time.

"Yeah!" The other kids holler.

"Toxic Town is so disgusting that it's shutting down," Bob adds. "They want to stop making Jumping Chocolate Caterpillars on Factory Street. The food is getting yucky and the light bulbs are out."

"It's so bad," Daisy agrees, "that our principal quit and the school has gone crazy."

"It's time for some superpowers," The Giz growls.

Use The Giz's Meat Vision to find a new principal on page 61
Use Coco's Amazing Tail Zap to find a new principal on page 62
Go Green in Lowe's Garden on page 67
Dig Deeper on page 66

You, Coco, and The Giz jump out of Dr. GreenWheels and follow Sheldon, the Psychic Cat, deep into the landfill. It's really hard to move. Sheldon pushes his eyeglasses up his nose. You wonder if the tape is going to hold them together.

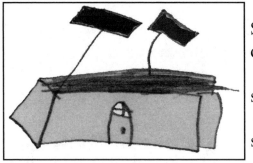

"Look at all this stuff," Sheldon says, his cape dragging in the muck.

Sheldon points to something in front of you.

"That's my cat house," he says.

It's the weirdest house you've ever seen. The walls are empty cardboard boxes that once held robots toys, cutie-pie stuffed animals, and video games. The windows are clear, plastic baggies with moldy, half-eaten, potato chips. The roof is made from old, white plastic bags with store names printed on the front.

"Come in," Sheldon says.

The four of you barely fit inside his garbage cat house. There's nothing much inside the house, except for a few bags of cat chow and a table made from old magazines. A bubble sits on the table.

"This is my magic bubble," Sheldon explains. "It helps me be a top psychic cat."

"Does it tell the future?" You ask.

"Yes," Sheldon replies. "It tells the future by showing what's happening now."

"I don't understand," Coco whimpers.

"Water," Sheldon shakes his head sadly. His big blue eyes close. His tail curls around the magic bubble.

"Water?" Coco asks.

"Water," Sheldon nods. The white fur on his back stands up. "Most people don't know what garbage does to water."

"Of course, we do," you say, sticking up for people.

Sheldon hisses. "No you don't. Water comes from a lot of places. It rains. Stuff in the landfill makes water. Then the water carries the poison from the garbage into rivers, lakes, and beaches."

"Then what happens?" You ask.

"It pollutes the water," Sheldon sighs. "Every day it gets worse."

"What will happen if it doesn't stop?" Coco asks.

Sheldon lifts one white paw, with a brown spot at the tip. He licks it clean and very gently, like only a cat can do and rubs the magic bubble.

Inside the magic bubble, a colorful playground appears. Kids play on a soccer field. Suddenly, they run over to the water fountain to get a drink. Instead of clear, cool water, brown, mucky stuff sprays into their faces.

"Ick!" You shout.

Sheldon rubs the bubble again. Now there's a beach. The sun is bright, the sky is blue, and there are no clouds. It's a perfect day for swimming. Kids rush to the water but stop short. There's a giant sign in the sand.

DIRTY WATER. NO SWIMMING ALLOWED.

The magic bubble changes again. It's Meadow Pond Park. The park is usually thick with trees and birds; the pond is busy with fish and frogs. You look closer. Everything has changed. The birds, frogs, and fish are gone. The pond is covered in green slime, and the trees have no leaves. There are lots of creepy crawlies.

"No!" you cry.

The Giz raises his big paw. "I'm going to pop your bubble and make that muck go away."

Sheldon howls. "You might get rid of the bubble, but it won't make the problem go away!"

The Giz snarls. "I'll make it all better. I'll use my Meat Vision to get rid of the garbage."

I'll use my Amazing Tail Zap to make things better," Coco yelps. She circles the magic bubble like it's a toy squirrel.

"Stuff it," Sheldon meows. "That won't work."

You look at Sheldon, Coco, and The Giz. Someone has to be right.

Which way do you want to go?

❀ ❀ ❀ ❀ ❀ ❀ ❀

Save the day with The Giz's Meat Vision on page 69
Check out Coco's Amazing Zap on page 70
Follow Sheldon on page 72

"Let's hit the skateboard," Parliament Cat howls. Her lime green eyes glow like aliens in a scary movie.

She flips her tail and the purple skateboard appears out of nowhere. It's an amazing skateboard - bigger than anything you've ever seen. The board is painted a deep, dark purple. Math facts and spelling words are hidden underneath. Three pointy cat-paw controls stick up. You, Coco, The Giz, and Parliament Cat can squeeze on it.

"You're going to meet the garbage critters," Parliament Cat says. "We're flying there."

The Giz woofs.

"What's a garbage critter?" you ask.

"They're evil-looking things," Parliament Cat says. "Some have heads like dump trucks with bulldozer feet. Others look like muddy jelly with snail's eyes. They're ugly, slimy, and squish when they move. Worms love to live on them."

You shiver.

"Worst of all," Parliament Cat hisses, "they can be right in front of your eyes. You won't even know it until they eat their favorite food . . . biomass."

"What's biomass?" Coco whimpers, hiding behind The Giz.

"Biomass," Parliament Cat says importantly, "is all the organic muck in the landfill. It's stuff like the string beans you didn't eat for dinner, the moldy leaves you stuck in a black plastic bag and left for the garbage truck, your little sister's old, wood blocks and . . . poop. When organic stuff rots, it gives off gas, mostly methane and carbon dioxide. Biomass makes garbage critters really gassy. They burp methane and carbon dioxide right into the air!"

"That's spooky," you shudder.

"It sure is," The Giz agrees. "It also makes the earth very unhappy."

"What about their . . . dessert?" Coco whines. "Do they put whipped cream and sprinkles on their biomass?"

You take out your reporter's e-pad. "I think I need to take notes," you say. You certainly don't want to write about the pictures in your head!

"Think of it like this," Parliament Cat yowls. "The more garbage people make, the more food for the garbage critters, and the more landfill gas they burp that pollutes the air."

The Giz nods. "The earth gets sicker because landfill gas makes global warming worse."

Coco dives into a pile of trash from someone's garden. She does a crazy dance and comes up for air, her face decorated with chunks of old lawn, crinkly leaves, and chewed-up branches. A pine cone dangles from her mouth.

"What's global warming?" she asks.

Parliament Cat shakes her head. "You call that a superhero?" she says to The Giz.

The Giz sighs. "A superhero-in-training," he woofs.

Parliament Cat flicks her tail. Like most cats, she's not in love with dogs. "I'll show you what global warming does to the earth." She sticks her nose in the air.

The Giz growls.

"All aboard," Parliament Cat adds quickly, jumping on the

purple skateboard.

You, Coco, and The Giz join her.

"Take off!" Parliament Cat howls.

Suddenly, the purple skateboard leaps from the landfill into the air. You grab onto the edge with both hands as it flies higher and higher. The wind rushes past your face and your heart beats wildly. You soar through white, puffy clouds. It's fun and scary!

"Wa-hoooooo," Parliament Cat shouts.

Coco and The Giz bark wildly into the wind.

Slowly, you get used to the wind in your face. You look down and see that you're flying really high, just like a bird. Your heart beats even faster and you hold on for dear life. A few birds fly by. They look at you, caw loudly, and continue on their way. Everyone up here in the clouds seems to be used to flying - except you!

Turn to the next page ➤

You begin to feel comfortable on this purple skateboard, even when Parliament Cat sticks out her paw to catch a passing bird. The birds are too smart to let a cat on a flying purple skateboard grab hold of them. They know that flying cats have to pay a lot more attention to clouds than birds.

"I'm going to tell you about global warming," Parliament Cat says as if you were still on the ground, in the middle of the landfill.

Coco doesn't listen. She's too busy trying to play tag with the birds.

The Giz holds his nose high, like a dog with his head out the car window. You wonder if he can smell any hamburgers.

"Global warming," Parliament Cat continues, "is when the earth gets hotter."

"That sounds good," you cry. "If it's hotter we can have longer summers, swim more at the beach, and eat more ice cream."

The Giz barks when he hears you say ice cream.

"Let me show you what happens when the earth gets hotter," Parliament Cat hisses.

The purple skateboard turns sharply. The air gets cold. Everything is snow white. You can even see your breath. You shiver. The dogs are happy because their brown, curly hair keeps them warm. You think about how nice it would be to have a built-in coat.

You look down and all you can see is ice.

"We're over the Arctic!" you cry.

"Yes," Parliament Cat says. "Do you see it melting?"

"That's crazy! How can the Arctic and the North Pole melt?" You yell.

41

"Look carefully," Parliament Cat says.

You don't have cat eyes, but you can see what she's talking about. Below you, huge chunks of ice break off into the water. The ice is melting.

"Why isn't it frozen?" you ask.

"It should be frozen, but gases from places like the landfills make the earth too hot. It's called global warming. It's like putting ice cubes in a cup of soup. They melt." Parliament Cat sighs.

"Look," The Giz points with his nose. "There are polar bears."

"They're stuck," Coco cries.

Coco is right. There's a polar bear stuck on a tiny piece of ice, that is floating in the water. The ice is melting and the polar bear has no where to go.

"The polar bears lose their home when there's not enough ice," Parliament Cat adds.

"Global warming changes the earth's weather," The Giz explains. "It's really bad for all of us. Animals lose their homes, food won't grow, and baby animals get hungry."

Suddenly, the skateboard changes direction. In minutes, it gets very hot - like a boiling day in summer, when the sun is burning. All you see is brown. It's a dry desert without any trees, water, or animals. "Global warming pushed the rain clouds away and made everything too hot here," Parliament Cat says. "Now the people and animals that live here have no water."

You shiver, even though it's so hot.

"Take a look at this," Parliament Cat howls. She steers the skateboard over a beautiful forest. It's filled with fire!

"The forest is burning down," you cry.

"Yes," Parliament Cat says sadly. "The snow melted very early because the earth became too hot. There wasn't enough water to keep it from catching fire."

"Global warming is really bad," you holler. "Let's get rid of those landfill gases and the garbage critters. We have to do it NOW."

🐾 🐾 🐾 🐾 🐾 🐾 🐾

Send the garbage critters up in smoke on page 75
Catch the garbage critters in action on page 77
Roll on over to the landfill to meet a fuzz ball on page 44

McFurry, the giant fuzz ball, does a crazy roll over a pile of rusty bicycles. "Follow me," he gurgles.

McFurry is the biggest giant fuzz ball you've ever seen. You wonder how he got so large and so clean. He bounces around the landfill like a sparkly white rabbit.

"I'm a clean green machine," McFurry explains, reading your thoughts. "I got this big because there's so much garbage." He disappears behind a pile of smelly, old socks.

"I'm here," he calls from the other side.

Coco leaps over the socks and buries her nose into McFurry's fuzz. McFurry laughs. "You're tickling me!"

You take out your reporter's e-pad. This is going to be a big story!

McFurry spins away from Coco and dives into a mountain of soggy shoeboxes, old, report cards, snotty tissues, and mucky egg cartons.

"Watch this!" McFurry opens his furry fuzz ball mouth and takes a big bite. He makes a weird gurgling sound, and the mountain of trash gets smaller.

"Wow!" you cry. "You ate all the garbage."

McFurry bounces into the air, does a flip, and lands right next to the mountain. His fur turns a dull white. Suddenly, he looks very sad for a giant fuzz ball. "In a few minutes the garbage will be back," he mumbles.

You look at the mountain. McFurry is right - the garbage is back.

"Yow," McFurry does a triple flip in the air. "Even worse," he burps, "if you wait a few more minutes, the mountain gets bigger."

You can't believe your eyes. The mountain of garbage is growing. "What can we do?" you holler.

McFurry zooms into the air, somersaults, and lands at your feet. "I might be a clean green machine, but I'm not big enough to stop all the garbage."

"Why can't we stop the garbage before it hits the landfill?" You ask.

No one says a word.

"Follow me," you holler. You know just where to go.

❀ ❀ ❀ ❀ ❀ ❀ ❀

Meet Mr. McRecycle on page 82
Meet Ms. HAPPYmeal on page 84

DIG DEEPER!

Landfills are an old-fashioned way of dealing with garbage. The first garbage dump was created over 2600 years ago!

Plastic can last more than one thousand years. That means the soda bottle you throw away, will be around way past the lifespan of your grandkids!

The average landfill holds 92 million pounds of toxic waste. That's about the same weight as 184,000,000 bags of potato chips! Anyone want to munch?

A landfill produces gas that pollutes the air. The gas is mostly methane and carbon dioxide. When a landfill closes, it continues to make gas for up to twenty years.

Every year, Americans throw out 24 million tons of leaves and grass clippings. Most of it goes to landfills, where it pollutes the air and water.

It's up to you. Which way do you want to go?

🐾 🐾 🐾 🐾 🐾 🐾 🐾

Peek into landfill future with Sheldon on page 35
Fly with Parliament Cat on her purple skateboard on page 38
Join McFurry on page 44
Check out Lowe's Garden on page 80

"Why does The Willow Pet Hotel have so much electric power when the other places are dark?" You ask.

Mr. Marc smiles proudly. "We get our electricity from the sun! It's called solar power. We have special panels on the roof that use sunlight to make electricity. We don't have to worry about burning dirty fuels to make electricity, like they do at the power plant. Solar power makes the earth happy and keeps the air clean."

Suddenly, you begin to cough. Your eyes water and you feel dizzy. Clouds of thick gray smoke surround you.

"It's a Dirty Energy Creep," Mr. Marc wails. "Help!"

You gasp. There's a hairy slug with pointy ears, a black tongue, and three eyes that change color. Slowly it faces you. It wears an evil, blood-red cape that says:

DON'T GO GREEN!

What's happening? You're choking mad! The only thing you know is that it's time to fight for green.

Fight Dirty Energy Creeps at the hotel on page 86
Fight Dirty Energy Creeps at the power plant on page 87
Write a law to fight Dirty Energy Creeps everywhere on page 91

You rush over to the giant freezer. A bowl of cotton candy ice cream will help you figure out how to write your news story. You can't wait - maybe you'll add chocolate syrup and whipped cream.

You open the freezer door and see lots of ice cream. Great! You read the flavors.

Rocky kibble and bits
Dog biscuits and cream
Turkey gravy fudge

Yuck! There's no way this ice cream is going to help you write your story!

The end of this gooey adventure.

DIG DEEPER!

Fossil fuels ruin our environment, just like homework ruins our day.

 Hydropower (water power) is a clean, renewable energy that currently provides about 19% of the electricity in the world. That's $10 for every $100 spent on electricity!

 Solar power captures the energy from the sun, after it makes its 8-minute trip of 93 million miles to earth and is turned into electricity. Now, that's traveling at the speed of light!

 Windmills have been used to do physical work, like crush grain and pump water. Now, they're used to make electricity

 Almost 4 tons of coal every year is used for each person in the United States.

It's up to you. Which way do you want to go?

🐾 🐾 🐾 🐾 🐾 🐾 🐾

Smell the flowers at Lowe's Green Garden on page 80
Follow Mr. Marc at The Willow Pet Hotel on page 86

Dr. GreenWheels rides the high road.

"Where are we going?" you ask.

"We're meeting at the GreenWheels' family lineup," he snaps. "There's a problem."

"What problem?"

"Hrmmmmph," Dr. GreenWheels says, not answering your question.

GreenWheels country is really nice. There are trees everywhere. You don't see any Bone Trees because they grow in HyBrid country. Instead, there are short, hairy Kibble Bushes.

There are more dogs on Gizco Island than you've ever seen in your life! The puppies play around the Kibble Bushes. The adult dogs roll on their backs, warming their bellies in the sun. They even drive cars! As you go by, the dogs bark a welcome to Coco and The Giz!

The GreenWheels' family lineup is in a big, grassy field. At the front of the field is a marble statue of Coco and The Giz. The statue is taller than a building! A few strange-looking birds sit happily on top of The Giz's marble head. You and Coco laugh.

Dr. GreenWheels stops in a crowd of cars. Coco and The Giz leap out of the car. You move slowly with only two legs. You're not sure what to expect. It looks like a living parking lot!

Suddenly, there's a roar of sirens, honks, engines revving, and strange machine sounds.

"That's a GreenWheels' family cheer," Dr. GreenWheels explains.

You don't know what to say. Instead, you smile and clap your hands.

Coco gets so excited she leaps into the air, chasing her tail. "Behave!" The Giz says and pins her down with his paw.

Three cars circle you.

"Meet EthoMobile GreenWheels," Dr. GreenWheels says. "We call her Ethie, for short."

Ethie is a small, bright red car with pretty paws and bones painted on her sides. She idles forward. "I'm Ethie," she says proudly, "because I only use ethanol for fuel. Ethanol is made mostly from corn and sugar cane. That means it's renewable - we can grow more of it every year."

The cars, behind Ethie, honk loudly.

"Yeah," Ethie hums, "and it's great for the earth."

The GreenWheels give her a noisy, family cheer.

The second car in the circle honks for silence. "I'm Oiler GreenWheels," he bellows. Oiler is a hulk with black, gray, and white muscles of steel. He can't stay still for a minute. Oiler zooms around the field as the GreenWheels' family cheers.

Oiler jams on his brakes. "My oil comes from earth-happy places - like soybean farms and food scraps. Some of my best stuff is recycled restaurant oil from French fries and coconut fried chicken. When I race, it smells like dinner!"

Coco starts to fire another Amazing Tail Zap, but The Giz

stops her with his paw.

"Not now, Coco-nutty," Dr. GreenWheels whispers.

The third car is dark blue and very sleek. She edges forward. "I'm Fuela GreenWheels," she says in a high voice. "I'm new - there aren't a lot of us. I use fuel cells to work. My fuel cells need hydrogen and oxygen, and when I'm finished racing, there's only water left."

You stare at Fuela.

"A lot of people don't know about me," she continues, "because most fuel cells are in spaceships."

The GreenWheels are very quiet. They really respect Fuela.

"Well," The Giz says finally, "how can we help?"

"Ethie, Oiler, and Fuela have no fuel," Dr. GreenWheels says. "Without fuel, the GreenWheels can't enter the Annual Bone Challenge Car Race, and," he adds, "they need a lot more than gas bubble gum spit."

Which way do you go?

❀ ❀ ❀ ❀ ❀ ❀ ❀

Search the farms with Ethie on page 92
Chew the fat with Oiler on page 93
Ride the rockets with Fuela on page 95

Make new friends at Lowe's Garden

Meet More Friends ➡

53

Coco and The Giz thank
the fourth grade Which Way student-authors

Alexander Farr
Alexandra Lyver
Alexis Vilela
Allison Casas
Amayah Toney
Amy Okano
Andrea Cabrera
Andrea James
Andrew Rosa
Antonia Mariano
Ariana Catania
Armani Prosper
Benjamin White
Bradley Licin
Brandon O'Neill
Brianna Chodash
Brianna Jones
Brieanna McCutcheon
Cairo Carter
Camila Polo
Cassandra Zangerle
Chloe Prosper
Christina Milord
Christine Galloway
Daniella Rampersad

Daniel Colloca
Darien Mercado
Devonte Green
Ederlyn Firpo
Edward Leonardo
Elizabeth Brunner
Emily Geary
Emily Nunez
Grecia Asencios
Hiah Saljooki
Hope Naber
Ian Leanza
Iqra Chohan
Jasaan Richardson
Jasmine Perkins
Jessica Kasenchak
John Meehan
Jonathan Link
Justin McCann
Kayla King
Kayla Rivera
Kevin Lema
Kiara Garcia
Kimberly Martinez
Kyle Gully

Lauren Becvar
Lydia Perez
Matthew Bercier
Melissa Getz
Nicholas Bruno
Nicholas Negron
Oscar Romero
Osman Rivera
Pamela Obando
Paul Beaumont
Robert Isoldi
Ryan Dennerlein
Samantha Yearwood
Samantha Cherry
Shaqueia Woods
Shiloe Gardner
Skye Prosper
Skylar Holst
Steffen Ivanish
Stephanie Dlugokencky
Tarik Patterson
Thomas Perry
Tyson Thompson
Zachary Zwerin
Zachary McGunnigle

You're off again! The sand on Gizco Island Beach blows in all directions as Dr. GreenWheels flies into the air.

"I thought we're here," you cry.

"People," Dr. GreenWheels grumbles, "they don't know anything. The smell of people just ruins my day."

Coco tries to use her Amazing Tail Zap to cheer up Dr. GreenWheels. First she tries to change a red rubber ball into a TV. She ends up with a dancing mouse in shiny gold sneakers. The superhero-in-training tries to change the dancing mouse into spaghetti and meatballs. She ends up with a mushy scrambled egg in a hat.

"At least you're trying, Coco-nutty," Dr. GreenWheels says kindly, "but that has got to go."

Dr. GreenWheels turns off his engine and starts spraying himself with *Petganics*, a Healthy Home Product made especially for dogs. He makes the smell of people leave the air.

Coco sniffs the air and claps her paws.

"We're headed for ThermaSip Village," The Giz interrupts, "where the HyBrids live. It's on the other side of the volcano."

You stare out the window at Gizco Island. It looks very different on the other side of the volcano. There are trees and hills everywhere. The beach is far away. The volcano is big and rocky, with lots of smoke coming from the top.

Dr. GreenWheels lands in ThermaSip Village Square, at the foot of the volcano.

"We're here," Dr. GreenWheels grumbles. "Out!"

You, Coco, and The Giz climb out of the car.

ThermaSip Village is the prettiest town you've ever seen.

Houses in all different colors and sizes surround the village square and nearby hills. The air smells sweet like fresh flowers. There are colorful birds and dogs everywhere.

"Wow!" You clap your hands.

ThermaSip Village is in one of the most beautiful places in the world. It's also in one of the most dangerous places in the world. The volcano causes regular earthquakes. A lot of storms and hurricanes come from the ocean beyond the village square. It gets very cold in the winter and super hot in the summer. With global warming, the storms and temperatures are much worse.

The HyBrids in ThermaSip Village live in the safest homes

in the world. They don't have to worry about earthquakes, storms, and hot and cold weather. Their houses save energy, use very little wood, and keep the earth happy. That's why they can live on the other side of the island. HyBrids like to make everyone . . . including the earth . . . feel really good.

"HyBrids are very peaceful," Dr. GreenWheels shifts gears. "They like to make everyone happy."

A pretty little orange car with a big yellow driving bubble steers across the village square and stops in front of you.

"I'm Rainbow," she whirs softly. "Prius is my first cousin."

"Who is Prius?" You ask.

"He's the best HyBrid ever," Rainbow says, turning bright gold. Rainbow is a transformer, just like Dr. GreenWheels. Instead of changing shapes, she changes colors. Her colors show how Rainbow feels.

"Prius has hybrid synergy drive," Rainbow explains. "That's why he can win the Bone Challenge."

For the first time ever, Dr. GreenWheels has run out of words. Coco and The Giz give him a very strange look.

"Can we meet Prius?" You ask.

I'll take you to him," Rainbow replies, turning bright red.

Dr. GreenWheels moves really close to Rainbow. "You can take me anywhere, baby." He says in a husky voice.

"I think he likes her," Coco whispers to you and The Giz.

It's amazing! Is cranky old Dr.GreenWheels falling in love with Rainbow?

You, Coco, and The Giz climb inside Dr. GreenWheels. He smells like chocolate Valentine's Day candy.

Rainbow leads you to her cousin's house. Prius has one of the nicest homes in ThermaSip village. It sits on the top of a big green hill. The backyard is the Bone Tree Forest. There are dogs everywhere, feasting on the tasty bones that grow in the trees. You've heard a lot of stories about how much HyBrids love dogs and Bone Trees. You wonder if HyBrids like people more than Dr. GreenWheels does.

🐾 🐾 🐾 🐾 🐾 🐾 🐾

Meet Prius HyBrid on page 96
Run to Lowe's Garden on page 53

Dr. GreenWheels heads for the gray part of the island.

It takes just a few minutes to drive into GasGuy country. The gray sky is called smog. Smog is yucky air pollution. When cars and trucks burn gasoline fuel, they give off smoke called emissions. These emissions make the air dirtier and the smog thicker.

It makes your eyes water and your nose run. They also make global warming or climate change much worse.

You stare out the window, expecting strange creatures, and . . . it looks just like home! There are a lot of cars, SUVs, minivans, and trucks. Kids and dogs are playing ball and tag.

"Where are we going?" you ask.

"We're meeting Shredder, the captain of the GasGuys team, in the Bone Challenge," The Giz explains.

Dr. GreenWheels honks angrily. "They don't have enough gas."

You look at all the cars around you. If these cars always burn gas, why isn't there enough for the race?

"I'll make some gasoline," Coco yaps, getting ready for her Amazing Tail Zap.

"No!" You, The Giz, and Dr. GreenWheels yell.

Coco looks hurt.

"You're a superhero-in-training, Coco-nutty," Dr. GreenWheels says kindly.

"I don't want any bubble gum spit in my hair," you add.

Dr. GreenWheels stops in front of a plain-looking driveway.

You see a deep blue car with rocket blasters on the back.

"That's Shredder," The Giz says.

There are two other cars with Shredder - Sham and Vampire.

"Shredder has a weird time clock," Dr.GreenWheels warns. "Watch out."

You, Coco, and The Giz climb out of Dr. Greenwheels.

"I'm Shredder," he says.

Coco does a crazy superhero-in-training dance. "Do you want to see my Amazing Tail Zap?" she asks.

"Are you racing in the Bone Challenge," The Giz asks before Shredder can reply.

"We want to," Shredder frowns, "but we can't. There's not enough gas to go around."

"I don't understand," you say. "All these cars use gas, so there must be plenty of it."

"That's what you think," Shredder says sharply. He sounds a little bit like Dr. GreenWheels. You wonder if Shredder likes humans. "Get in my car and I'll show you," Shredder adds.

🐾 🐾 🐾 🐾 🐾 🐾 🐾

Drive to the source with Shredder on page 97
Make new friends at Lowe's Garden on page 53

DIG DEEPER!

The first mass produced car was the Model T Ford in 1908. It could run on gasoline, ethanol, or a combination of the two.

We need to conserve our fossil fuels like gasoline. If we don't, they'll become extinct like the dinosaurs - before we get a replacement. Then what will we do?

Your car will like renewable fuels, as much as you like hamburgers and French fries!

Sugar cane can be used to make ethanol to fuel cars. That's the same stuff used to make jellybeans.

A hybrid car uses gasoline and electricity. Some hybrids have an electric battery that recharges itself. Other hybrids plug into an electric outlet.

It's up to you. Which way do you want to go?

🐾 🐾 🐾 🐾 🐾 🐾 🐾

Race with the GreenWheels on page 50
Speed with the HyBrids on page 55
Rush with the GasGuys on page 58
Make new friends at Lowe's Garden on page 53

The Giz watches Rocky, the custodian, stacking tables and chairs into neat rows.

"You won't like this, Rocky," The Giz says. "We need to mess up your rows. I'll use my Meat Vision to change the lunchroom tables into a new principal."

The Giz takes a deep breath and looks at the tables and chairs. Suddenly . . . all the tables and chairs turn into a mountain of clean hamburgers.

The kids dive into the hamburgers, smearing ketchup all over the place.

Everyone knows that a good principal isn't made of hamburgers and ketchup.

The end of this meaty adventure.

"What kind of principal do you want for your school?" Coco asks the kids.

"She should be kind, sweet, and love the earth," Daisy says.

"She should be cool, funny, and magical," Bob nods.

"I'm going to use my Amazing Tail Zap to get just what you want," Coco yaps.

"No!" you and The Giz cry.

It's too late.

Coco fires her Amazing Tail Zap at the computer screen. Suddenly, a purple alien principal, with eight arms, appears.

The principal says something in a strange Martian language.

Bob and Daisy stare at the alien who could be a creature from outer space. "I don't think she will work," Bob says slowly.

"I got it," Coco barks. She fires her Amazing Tail Zap at the Martian principal.

You close your eyes. The Giz turns away. What will Coco come up with next?

"Meet Principal CeeKay," Coco says proudly. "She's the greatest, greenest principal in the whole world! I would even let her paint my tail string bean green," Coco giggles.

Everyone stares at the new principal.

Principal CeeKay looks . . . normal. She even speaks English, not Martian. "I hear you have problems," she says kindly.

Everyone nods.

"I think I can change things," Principal CeeKay nods. She reaches into her pocket and takes out her Mother Nature's Sunglasses. They have magic buttons on the sides.

Principal CeeKay puts on the glasses. "Let's get this school under control," she says and pushes a button.

Suddenly there's a loud noise. It sounds like hundreds of kids all plopping into chairs at the same time.

Principal CeeKay pushes another button on her sunglasses. A skinny plastic man with arms and legs suddenly appears.

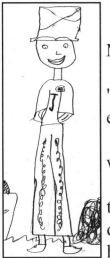

"Meet Johnson Diversey," she says proudly.

You look at the strange thing. "Who are you, Mr. Diversey?" you ask.

"I'm a green cleaner," Mr. Diversey explains. "I get rid of yuck in buildings and make the earth happy because I'm biodegradable."

"What's bio . . . de . . .," Coco can't say the word.

Mr. Diversey laughs. "Biodegradable means that stuff like cleaning fluid will decay or break down to become part of the earth without ever harming it."

"Wow!" Coco yaks.

"Do your thing," Principal CeeKay says to Mr. Diversey.

Out of nowhere, there's a flash of bright green. Mr. Diversey runs through the school, cleaning up all the moldy, orange jelly sandwiches, waffles with muddy butter, squashed jellybeans, and banana peels. All the yuck is gone! Toxic Town School is so clean that it smells just like fresh daisies!

Everyone claps and cheers Mr. Diversey and his biodegradable cleaning power.

"Now that Toxic Town School is back in order," Principal CeeKay says, "we have a big job ahead."

"What?" you ask.

"We have to clean up the whole town," Principal CeeKay replies, "so it won't shut down."

"How?" Daisy wails.

Principal CeeKay grins. "We need to make our own magic," she explains. "When kids take action, a lot can happen."

"Let's do it!" you cry.

"Great!" Principal CeeKay answers. "We'll need some green wizards to give us a hand."

Green wizards use their powers to make the earth happy.

They love when kids take action to clean up the planet. Which Green Wizard do you want to meet?

❀ ❀ ❀ ❀ ❀ ❀

E-Wiz, The Transformer Techie Wizard on page 102
Luna, the Cool Wizard on page 103
Eco-Nick, the Tasty Wizard on page 107

Hall of Green Wizards

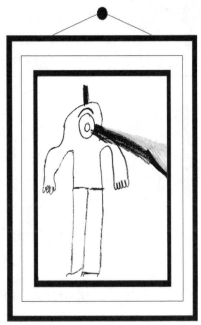

Beautiful flowers can be grown with compost made from rotten apples, banana peels, and last night's string beans.

Nearly half the money you pay for food is the cost of packaging. That means, if you pay $200 for all the food in your shopping cart, $100 is paid for wrappers. Think of what you could do with the extra $100!

The average household spends about $2,520 on gasoline in one year. That's about ten thousand flavored gum balls.

Every Sunday, Americans waste 90% of the newspapers that they could recycle. This uses up more than 500,000 trees.

Each American uses the equivalent of one, 100-foot tree a year in things like paper, furniture, toys, and wood products.

It's up to you. Which way do you want to go?

❀ ❀ ❀ ❀ ❀ ❀ ❀

Help the planet with Keyspan Energy on page 157
Find a new principal on page 62

Go Green at Lowe's Garden!

Meet more friends on the next page ➡

Coco and The Giz thank the
second grade Which Way student-authors

Abraham Pierre
Alexa Rae Munoz
Alexandra Khan
Aliaksadra Shkuratava
Allison Michelini
Alyssa Torres
Andrea Rua Llano
Ania Smith
Anthony Gardner
Arslan Khurram
Ashley Hunter
Brandon Smith
Charles Szomoru
Christina Green
Christopher Bermudez
Christopher Coalman
Christopher Johnson
Deanna Knipfing
De'Ontrae Green
Devon Hicks

Dilwar Zaman
Dylan DaPonte
Elvis Diaz
Enesa Omerovic
Eneysshia Smith
Giavonni Passanante
Ginamarie Curto
Hailey Bianca
Imani Jackson
Jared Iudica
Jasmine Rogers
Johnathan Brewster
Jonathan Brunner
Jordan Campbell
Joseph Costantino
Julia Ferranto
Julia Randazzo
Kailynn Dean
Karissa Cerullo
Khylil Mixon
Kriston Williams
Maliya Rodriguez
Mariam Duvesh

Megan Tannacore
Michael Green
Mikayla Balthazar
Nicholas Elliot
Nicholas Feltman
Olivia Colloca
Peter Giammona
Rebecca Innes
Renee Prince
Romeo Guzman Portillo
Ryan Cherry
Ryan Vitzhum
Saif Cakirlar
Samantha Uebel
Sean Sheridan
Sha-Asia Carr
Shakeira Davis
Sophia Borga
Tamara Tyvylik
Victoria Addesso
Zyn Dasha Farris

The Giz is ready to go! He stands straight up and looks around the landfill. His brown eyes get big, round, and scary looking. The Giz stares as hard as he can at a big pile of old milk cartons. Pow! He hits it with his Meat Vision!

The milk cartons change into a huge pile of hamburgers.

"That's great," You shout. "You can give the hamburgers to people around the world and stop world hunger!"

"Wait," Coco shouts. "Look around. You can't make all the garbage into meat. There's too much of it."

The Giz pauses, hamburgers falling out of his mouth.

It looks so good that you grab a hamburger, too.

Tons and tons of meat start to fall all around you. People and dogs won't eat it fast enough. You shiver at the thought of so many rotten hamburgers.

Coco hangs her head. "I don't think that Meat Vision will solve the problem," she whimpers.

The end of this meaty idea.

🐾 🐾 🐾 🐾 🐾 🐾 🐾

Sniff your way to a new path on page 72

69

Coco has been practicing her Amazing Zap. "I'm ready," she yaps. "Can you see the large, flat boat that ships garbage? It's right over there in the ocean, with nothing on it."

"Watch out," The Giz says to you.

Coco does a little doggie dance and faces a pile of dented soda cans. She fires her Amazing Tail Zap

The Giz waits patiently.

The pile of soda cans is dumped onto the barge.

"Yes!" Coco yaps happily. "The dented soda cans are gone. I can zap all the garbage to the barge. There won't be anymore landfill."

You and The Giz look at each other.

"Where's the barge taking the soda cans?" you ask gently.

Coco rubs her head. "I know!" She yelps. "It's going to Garbage Island."

"Superheroes have to think," The Giz growls. "You're just moving trash from one place to another. It doesn't get rid of it."

"Maybe," you say slowly, "people could recycle the soda cans. Then you wouldn't have to send them anywhere."

Suddenly, Dr. GreenWheels appears. His nap is over. "People," he says in a cranky voice, "can recycle a lot of things to get rid of garbage. They don't. What can you expect from brainless, two-legged humans?"

You open your mouth to defend people.

"Look," The Giz barks. "The big pile of dented soda cans is back!"

"See," Dr. GreenWheels grumbles, "your Amazing Zap just makes room for more garbage. It's a bottomless pit of trash. You didn't solve the problem."

The end of this bottomless pit of trash

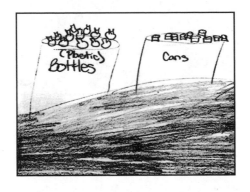

❀ ❀ ❀ ❀ ❀ ❀ ❀

Snooze at Lowe's Garden on page 80
Play with a giant fuzz ball on page 44

Sheldon rubs his magic bubble. "Maybe the bubble can tell us something about the environment."

"That's a big word for a bubble," Coco yelps.

"The environment is everything around us," Gizmo woofs. "It's more than the bubble."

"The environment includes the soil, water, plants, people, and animals," Sheldon adds.

You, Coco, and The Giz stare into the bubble.

There's a place inside. You lean closer. Yes! It's your home town. There are three dancing R's.

"R's?" you cry. "How can an R help? It's only a letter."

Sheldon purrs happily. "They're the Three R's of the Environment."

"What's that?" you ask, as you write it on your reporter's e-pad.

"I know," Coco barks. "The Three R's of the Environment stand for Red licorice, Racing caterpillars, and Roaring mice."

The Giz shakes his head. "You want to try again?" he asks Coco.

Sheldon laughs. "The Three R's of the Environment stand for Reduce, Reuse, and Recycle. They tell us what we can do to help the landfill problem." Sheldon meows. "When we help the landfills, we keep our water clean and make our planet happy. The future of the earth is in **your** hands!"

"Do you mean that I should give my old squeaky toy to the puppy down the street, instead of throwing it out?" Coco yelps.

"Yes," Sheldon says, "that's just what I mean. If you reuse things like your squeaky toy and the plastic milk bottles from the refrigerator, they won't go to the landfill, where it can take up to 1000 years to decompose."

"Do they really compose or make music at the landfill?" Coco giggles.

"No! Decompose means to rot," The Giz explains. "Your squeaky toy and the plastic milk bottles will stay around in the landfill for hundreds of years. Why throw them out? We should turn them into something useful!"

"Plastic milk bottles make really good chew toys," Coco yaps.

"Used, plastic jars are great for my pens," you add.

"Yes," Sheldon says. "Here's how it works."

He speaks slowly in a soft cat voice. "You can reduce or make less garbage by giving away your old toys, clothes, and books to other people who can use them. One kid's garbage is another kid's treasure - and a lot less trash goes to the landfill."

"Hand-me-downs make the earth happy," you cry.

"Right," Sheldon says. "Recycling stuff also makes the earth happy. There's a factory right here that uses plastic bags and old soda bottles to make plastic wood for furniture, sun decks, and fences!"

You think about all the plastic bottles and bags that are thrown away, just in your own town.

Sheldon, as a psychic cat, reads your thoughts. "If you recycle just one soda bottle, there's less garbage in the landfill - and you save enough energy to power your television for six of your favorite shows!"

"We could still swim at the beach and drink water from the fountain," Coco interrupts.

The Giz grins, "And we could keep all those great birds and fish in our pond."

"The Three R's are magic," Coco yelps.

You, Coco, and The Giz know that the landfills would be smaller and the water would be cleaner if people, dogs, and cats used the Three R's everyday. You have the superpower to change the future!

Now that's a great story for *Book Web News*!

🐾 🐾 🐾 🐾 🐾 🐾 🐾

See the Three R's in action on page 110
Follow the paper trail on page 114
Become a water buddy on page 163

Parliament Cat slows the flying, purple skateboard. "I know where the garbage critters hang out," she says softly.

"Cool," you holler. "We can help stop global warming!"

"I can use my Amazing Tail Zap," Coco snarls. "I'll turn them into jellybeans that we can squash."

The Giz shakes his head. "You're a superhero," he snarls. "Use your head!"

"I have a better idea," you laugh. "The Giz can use his Super Sniffer to find them and his Super Strength to get rid of them."

"Now we're talking," Coco adds. "I'll zap them into marble statues and put them in museums around the world."

"Wait!" The Giz woofs. "Why don't we zap them into outer space?"

"Mmmmm," Coco says thoughtfully. "We can send them to Mars and Jupiter, where the aliens eat garbage critters for breakfast."

"Stop!" Parliament Cat howls. "That stuff won't work."

"Why?" you ask.

"Garbage critters are smart . . . not like a dumb superhero-in-training. They're all over the planet. People make so much garbage that as soon as we get rid of one landfill's garbage critters, there are zillions of them ready to take their place."

"So what can we do?" you ask.

"Look," Parliament Cat hisses.

You look at the landfill. There are hundreds of garbage critters hanging out on a pile of white, supermarket plastic bags. It's as big as a lake.

"Here's what you do," Parliament Cat howls. She steers the

75

purple flying skateboard right into the garbage critters. She opens her mouth as wide as possible. Like a dragon guarding a castle, Parliament Cat shoots fire at the garbage critters.

Suddenly, you're choking. It's really hard to breathe. The burning garbage critters are starting to float into the air. There are more and more of them floating around. They are polluting the air with smoke!

Parliament Cat gags. "Heck," she coughs, "this always kicks up my asthma."

It's really clear. Burning trash is not the way to get rid of garbage critters. However, it is a good way to pollute the air and make people, dogs, and cats sick.

You reach the end of this smoky adventure. All you have to show for the day is a whopper of a cough. Go home and take a shower for a wet ending!

🐾 🐾 🐾 🐾 🐾 🐾

Try again on page 77
Meet the Keyspan Kids on page 169

"Let's think," Parliament Cat says. "What's the best way to get rid of garbage critters?"

"I feel bad for them," Coco yelps. "It's not their fault that they eat biomass and burp landfill gas. The garbage critters don't make garbage - people do."

You start to say something, but the words don't come. You can't stick up for people this time!

The Giz looks at you with his big, round brown eyes. "Maybe Coco can use her Amazing Tail Zap to change the garbage critters into something good," he says thoughtfully.

You're not quite sure that you trust Coco's Amazing Tail Zap. She could make a mistake and end up with a zillion gummy worms.

"Can you make them into healthy food?" you ask quietly.

"Only aliens eat garbage critters for lunch," Coco frowns.

"What about collecting all the garbage in the world, melting it into car fuel, bottles, clothes, and paper, and giving it to the poor?" you suggest.

"We can make it into fish," Parliament Cat licks her lips.

". . . and cheeseburgers," The Giz adds.

"Turkey gravy ice cream," Coco licks her lips.

Suddenly, you hear a threatening voice. "Land this skateboard, now!"

You look over the edge of the skateboard. You're not flying very high anymore. In fact, you're hovering right over a hill of old telephone books in the landfill. A big, strong policeman is right below you.

"Now," he commands.

Parliament Cat slowly lands on the telephone books.

"I'm Officer George," the policeman says sternly.

You, Parliament Cat, Coco, and The Giz look guilty.

"Do you have a license to fly this thing," Officer George asks Parliament Cat.

"Of course," Parliament Cat says in a huffy voice. "I would never fly a skateboard without a license."

Everyone knows that police like to talk to people more than strange dogs and cats.

"We're looking for a way to get rid of the garbage critters," you interrupt.

Officer George shakes his head. "Don't get rid of them," he says. "Take care of the critters, and they'll make the earth happy. It's called garbage critters-to-energy."

Your heart starts to pound. "Can garbage critters really be good?"

"Just put them to work," Officer George replies.

🐾 🐾 🐾 🐾 🐾 🐾 🐾

Watch the garbage critters at work on page 113
Eat dinner with the critters on page 115

Coco and The Giz thank the kindergarten Which Way student-authors

Aaliyah Green
Alexa Haas
Alexis Rubio
Allanah Zwiebel
Angela Huang
Anthony Serpenti
Anton Green
Bella Cincotta
Bobby Lorne Shepherd
Brian Primm
Britney Huang
Brittney Lyver
Cassandra Santiago
Christian Lella
Clara Szomoru
Connor Dyckman
Daisha Little
Daniel Maldonado
Daniel Meyers
David Schneider
DeAndre Irving
Elijah Morinville
Eric Willsen
Farrah Roesch
Frank Toney
Gabriella LaManna
Gavin Kalista
George Miller

Gregory O'Neill
Hailey Rose Nunez
Haven Johns
Hijab Nasir
Iqra Baig
Jacob Lesko
James Feltman
James Marinos
Jayden Smith
Jayna Schmidt
John Picciano
John Rivera
Jonathan Cine
Jordi Diaz
Josef Moses
Joseph Hefline
Joseph Shepherd
Julianna Camargo
KaShaun Boyd Perkins
Kayla Monroe
Lauryn Berger
Leigh Harris
Lela Omerovic
Lily Meehan
Lucas Bercier
Madeline Jordan
Marina Churchillo
Marycecilia Mastronardi

Mehak Chohan
Melinda Kayku
Melissa Link
Melissa Okano
Michael Brown
Michael Coccaro
Michael Guigliano
Mikasia Jones
Naima Cakirlar
Naomi Shepherd
Nicholas Fioravanti
Nileah Fulmore Williams
Pardeep Kaur
Paul Smith
Peter Lopez
Roxanne Zwerin
Samuel Fernandez
Sara Bianca
Sean Johnson
Sean Daniel Johnson
Tia Coltrain
Tian Coltrain
Veronica Guardado
Victoria Churchillo
Victoria Hunter
Victoria Schmahl
Zachary Iudica

Welcome to Lowe's Garden

Meet more friends on the next page ➜

Coco and The Giz thank the
fifth grade Which Way student-authors

Aldwin James
Alexa Marinos
Ali Noor
Alyssa White
Angelica Iacono-Henderson
April Franchi
Brendan Henriquez
Brittnie DiSalvo
Bruno Souza
Carly Heinlein
Charles Carter
Cheryl Posner
Christian Miller
Christie Conk
Christopher Romero
Christopher Gardner
Christopher Roman Serra
Connor Shires
Daina Walshe
Damian Yodice
Danaizia Pitt
Danielle Hagemeyer
Dean Cicciari
Dominique Chodash
Edward Bisson
Elhum Saljooki
Elijah Andrews
Emily Garren
Emily Scheuer
Erin Campbell
Fabienne Edouard

Felicia Lopez
Frank Piccione
Frank Baranek
Gabriella Buckley
Gabrielle Bryson
Gabrielle Davolia
Gerald Archie
Hailey Sluszka
Ilaisiah Brooks
Imani Muhammad
Isaiah Hiciano
Ivette Aybar
Jamison Sherretts
Janely Acevedo
Jessica Haas
Jeydi Ramirez
John Hurta
John Pisarczyk
Jonaiah Webster
Jonathan Demetriou
Joseph Baker
Joseph Dubanos
Joseph Giglia
Kayla Kohlhepp
Kevin Bell
Kevin Baietto
Kevin White
Kevin Leonardo
Kimberly Leonardo
Kyle Williams
Marlen Hernandez
Marisa Kerrigan
Megan Diaz

Mel-Shawn McPherson
Michelle Heinlein
Michelle Eichinger
Miguel Moreno
Nicholas Tannacore
Noah Buffins
Paul Enciso
Philip Catania
Punam Kaur
Rachel Rex
Raymond Hilker
Robert DeClara
Roni Lema
Saad Ullah Khan
Samantha Altamirano-Castillo
Sapphira Haber
Sarah Carr
Savannah Parker Davis
Sergio Polidori
Shane Tyson
Sharizma Budden
Shawn Bremner
Stephanie Bianca
Steven Lenzy
Tamara Simpson
Tessa Avolin
Toni-Ann Martorano
Tyler Winn

Mr. McRecycle is a really cool guy. He looks a little bit like Ronald McDonald without the red stripes and clown face. He sits on a bench, munching apple dippers.

"How can I help you?" Mr. McRecycle asks. He's a little surprised when he sees you, two dogs, and a giant fuzz ball. Mr. McRecycle is very polite, so he pretends there's nothing strange going on.

"You're the greatest recycler in the world!" You say. "You're famous. Can you help McFurry stop the garbage before it gets to the landfill?"

Mr. McRecycle shakes his head. "It's not easy," he begins, "but I do it everyday. The trick is to get people to change their habits."

"How?" McFurry babbles.

"You need to make people become green clean machines, just like you," Mr. McRecycle replies.

You know what Mr. McRecycle is saying. A long time ago no one ever thought about garbage. Mr. McRecycle changed that. Now he spends over one hundred million dollars buying recycled materials - stuff that never reaches the landfill.

Mr. McRecycle laughs. "Our orange juice used to come in ready-to-serve containers. Now it ships frozen. We send four million pounds *less* garbage to the landfill!"

"Wow!" McFurry bubbles. "That's a lot of giant fuzz balls."

"No one even knows," Mr. McRecycle adds, "that our Happy Meal boxes, carryout bags, carryout trays, and napkins are all made from recycled paper."

"Can you imagine," McFurry coos, "if everyone did that."

"Now you're thinking like a real clean green machine," Mr. McRecycle roars. "That's just the beginning."

"Why don't we have some hamburgers and talk about it?" The Giz barks.

Everyone agrees but you. You would rather have Chicken McNuggets!

🐾 🐾 🐾 🐾 🐾 🐾 🐾

Check out McRecycle's clean place on page 117

Ms. HAPPYmeal looks like a pretty paper bag with skinny arms and legs.

McFurry eyes pop. "Ok, I know I'm just a giant fuzz ball, but how can a paper bag help make less garbage?"

Ms. HAPPYmeal giggles. "It's right in front of your eyes."

"I only see hamburger," The Giz snarls.

"I'll take the fries," Coco woofs.

"Before you eat anything," Ms. HAPPYmeal says, "look at my paper bag."

You look at the bag. It's filled with cool designs and puzzles. "What about it?" You ask.

"You missed it!" Ms. HAPPYmeal cries. She stands on her head, which is not very easy for a paper bag. On her bottom is a small black circle of arrows. You lean closer.

"You're made from recycled paper!" You shout.

Ms. HAPPYmeal flips up and does a quick dance. "Now look at my napkin."

It's hard to read. Finally you see the words: made from recycled paper.

Ms. HAPPYmeal smiles proudly. "We spend over one hundred million dollars a year on recycled stuff that doesn't go to the landfill."

"Arf," The Giz says.

"That's not all," Ms. HAPPYmeal adds. "We save trees from being cut down. See the hamburger?"

You can't really see the hamburger because The Giz ate it when no one was looking.

"A lot of people destroy rainforests so they can raise beef. Rainforests make the earth very happy. We won't use beef that comes from places where the rainforest has been cut down."

84

"I bet there's nothing green about the French fries," you say.

"Wrong!" Ms. HAPPYmeal giggles. "We used to get 36 pounds of French fries in a case. Now we pack 39 pounds per case. That's two million pounds less packaging a year, thrown into the landfill!"

McFurry spins around like a very happy giant fuzz ball. "If everyone did all those things we would have a lot less garbage in the landfill."

"Right!" Ms. HAPPYmeal shouts.

Ms. HAPPYmeal cuddles up to McFurry. She really likes him!

"You're beautiful," McFurry coos.

McFurry gives Ms. HAPPYmeal a big juicy kiss.

"We can tell everyone," Ms. HAPPYmeal purrs.

You, Coco and The Giz agree. McFurry is in love!

The Willow Pet Hotel is under attack. There are Dirty Energy Creeps everywhere. They all look different.

Smokefish, a wrinkled, smelly Dirty Energy Creep with long pink teeth, gets into your face. You push him and he changes into thick, gray smoke with tiny flecks of coal.

SlugCreep, with knife claws, green moldy body, and feet of steel is right behind Smokefish.

SlimyRock moves forward. His goblin eyes bulge from a head of garbage; his squishy lips are made of poop.

You can't fight them all!

"Mr. Marc," you yell. "What can we do?"

Suddenly, the lights go out. You can't see anything. All of the dogs, cats, and Dirty Energy Creeps are very quiet. Your heart races wildly.

Which way do you go?

Tackle the Dirty Energy Creeps on page 119
Search for Mr. Marc on page 122
Stop the ice cream from melting on page 124

The Dirty Energy Creeps are all over the place!

You can tell that it's really not a trick. You, Coco, and The Giz rush outside into the parking lot. It's really dark. Suddenly, a Dirty Energy Creep runs by. He has blue hair, slime feet, and a pointy, pink hat with red-hot sparkles. Coco leaps at him.

She misses.

The Dirty Energy Creep gets away, but his cap falls on the ground. Coco attacks the pink hat, sending red-hot sparkles in all directions. She gets so dizzy that she flops on the ground.

You and The Giz watch quietly.

"Good job," The Giz shakes his head, "you told that hat who's boss."

Coco yelps.

"Come on, Coco-nutty," Dr. GreenWheels honks gently. "It's time to get the bad guys at the power plant."

Coco and The Giz leap inside Dr. GreenWheels. You barely get your legs inside as Dr. GreenWheels turns on his lights and leaves The Willow Pet Hotel parking lot. You see lots of tiny, black pieces floating in the air.

"What are these black things?" you ask.

"Tiny flecks of coal that pollute the air," The Giz replies. He points to the power plant. Huge smokestacks send thick,

gray smoke into the air. All around you are wires that carry the electricity made at the power plant.

"The Dirty Energy Creeps burn coal to make steam," The Giz says. "The steam runs machines that make electricity. The electricity travels through the wires, until it reaches the wire that goes into your house."

You shake your head. They don't have to use coal to make electricity. They can use clean energy, like sun and wind. The Dirty Energy Creeps **love** coal.

"We'll get them," Coco growls, the pink hat still in her mouth. She sounds more like a creaky door than a superhero-in-training.

Dr. GreenWheels stops in front of the power plant. Something is very wrong. There's more gray smoke than ever before. The air smells like fire. You cough and your eyes burn. You, Coco, and The Giz get out of Dr. GreenWheels. It's your job to figure out what's going on. You make sure your reporter's e-pad is ready. This is going to be a big story.

There's a threatening sign on the front door.

Ms. Fossil Face is fired.

The Dirty Energy Creeps run this place now!

A shiver runs down your back.

"Which way?" you cry to Coco and The Giz.

❀ ❀ ❀ ❀ ❀ ❀ ❀

Search for Ms. Fossil Face on page 126
Track down The Dirty Energy Creeps on page 128
Shut down the power plant on page 132

Have fun at Lowe's Garden!

Meet more friends on the next page ➡

Coco and The Giz thank the third grade Which Way student-authors

Adam Farr
Ailyn DeMarco
Alyssa Manago
Amanda Liantonio
Amanda Galloway
Angela Mazzoli
Anthony Centamore
Ashley Boyd
Ashley Cleator
Ashley Dean
Ashley Murphy
Brenden Brady
Brenna Cicciari
Cameron Baker
Cevin Felix
Conor Thiele
Daniel Posner
Danielle Bolton
Danielle Falsetta
Danielle Levine
Danny Sawan
David DeClara
Devin DeRiso
Deyani Smith
Donte Osani
Dylan Towey
Emily Haggerty
Erykah Russell
Genesis Genao

Gianmarco Asencios
Gregory Phillips
Ilini Gamble
Jack Shires
Jamie O'Neill
Jamie Elliot
Jason Cooper
Jason Brown
Jessica Cortina
Jessica Chiu
Jonathan Porrata
Joseph Klages
Joseph Kase
Justen O'Neill
Kelsey Winn
Kenneth Heyman
Khadija Ali
Kiara Anderson
Kristopher Krupski
Kyle Ries
Kymberly Rambazis
Lavender Charlton
Madison Stigliano
Madison Kalista
Marcus Murray
Matthew Muller
Maya Joyner
Melquan Riggsbee
Michael Morinville

Natalie Kanaan
Nathan Guardado
Nicholas Passanante
Nicholas Benavides
Nina Eleanor Malusay
Olivia Thomas
Oriana Onorato
Pia Myers
Rachel Johns
Rawal Zaman
Rhiannon Callahan
Rohit Kumbhar
Ryan Arthur
Ryan Thompson
Sana Sabir
Sibel Gucum
Skylar Marinos
Stephanie Dubanos
Stephan Green
Sydney Rotunno
Tayla Fitzroy
Treionna Beavers
Tyler Rodriguez
Yoanne Romero
Yvonne Iqbal
Zachary Thomas
Zenobia McGhee

Your friends write laws to fight the Dirty Energy Creeps. Which one do you like best?

*People must recycle and use clean energy. If they don't, they will be sent to a special school to learn how to live in a clean environment.

*All Dirty Energy Creeps have to clean up their mess and then move out of town!

*Everyone has to put solar panels on the roof and chase away the Dirty Energy Creeps.

*If you use dirty energy, you have to go to military school.

*You have to use solar, wind, and water energy, instead of coal to make electricity.

*Recycle or go to a school that teaches you how to be good. Which way do you go?

🐾 🐾 🐾 🐾 🐾 🐾 🐾

Write your own law and email it to:
www.greenlaws@bookwebpublishing.com
We'll put your law online!

Check out the Keyspan Kids on page 169

Tears run down Ethie's windshield. "I'm everyone's darling car," she rumbles. "I know I can win the Bone Challenge!"

Ethie uses her windshield wiper to clear the tears.

"What's wrong?" You pat her hood.

"Something very bad has happened." Ethie idles her engine. "I'm stuck here with very little fuel. I can't find ethanol anywhere on Gizco Island. I can't race without more fuel."

Ethanol is usually made from corn, sugar cane, and other crops. Ethanol can also come from straw, wood chips, and corn stalks. There are cars that run on a mix of ethanol and gasoline. Ethanol has been used as a fuel for more than one hundred years. So why can't Ethie get ethanol?

"I know what to do!" You shout

"Get in!" Ethie revs up her engine.

You, Coco, and The Giz jump into Ethie and zoom down the fast lane.

Which way do you go?

🐾 🐾 🐾 🐾 🐾 🐾 🐾

Pop down to the corn farm on page 134
Detour to the sugar cane farm on page 135
Ride the fast lane to the landfill on page 136

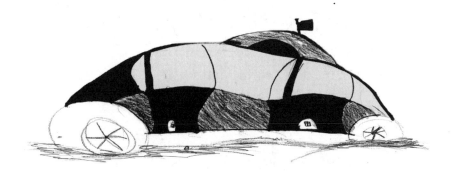

You, Coco, and The Giz climb inside Oiler.

You head for the soybean farm. It's closed for the race. You stare at the building that makes fuel oil from soybeans. It's amazing that people and cars can use the same fuel!

"Do people like soybeans?" Oiler asks.

"People love soybeans," you reply. "Most of the time they don't know they're eating them."

"I never saw soybeans in my bowl," Coco says.

"Dogs eat a lot of soybeans," you laugh. "Soy is in dog food and dog biscuits. Soy is also in soy sauce, cookies, and muffins for people."

"Wow!" Oiler honks.

"Soy can be used to make healthy crayons and ink," you add.

". . . and fuel," Oiler grumbles. "Let's go to Main Street," Oiler suggests. "If I can't get soybean oil from the farm, maybe I can pick up some oil that's left over from restaurant cooking."

You, Coco, and The Giz climb inside Oiler. He's really different from Dr. GreenWheels. Instead of a lot of gadgets, Oiler has large TV screens filled with pictures of the local restaurants, landfills, and soybean oil plants. They tell him when he can make an oil pick-up.

Now all of the screens have the same words written across the pictures . . .

CLOSED FOR THE BONE CHALLENGE

You shiver. You don't think that Oiler has a good chance of finding fuel. Oiler drives over to Main Street anyway.

Joseph's Fried Toe Nails Restaurant is closed.
Michelle's Candy Soy World is closed.
Norann's Fried Vegetables is closed.

You turn to Coco and The Giz. "Can you use your superpowers to make some French fries?" you suggest.

Coco and The Giz look at each other.

"We don't know how to cook," Coco whimpers. "We never went to cooking school."

Which way do you go?

🐾 🐾 🐾 🐾 🐾 🐾

Smell the flowers at Lowe's Garden on page 53
Sniff out the landfill with Ethie on page 136
Meet a real truck that collects cooking oil for fuel on page 139

You, Coco, and The Giz climb inside Fuela. She's very strange. She looks more like a spaceship than a car. Fuela's screens are filled with pictures of stars and planets. You see a robot arm and a space-to-earth workstation.

Fuela needs some new fuel cells. You, Coco, and The Giz look at each other. Everyone knows that spaceships and their fuel cells don't come from Gizco Island! Spaceships use fuel cells, and they don't pollute the air. Dr. Greenwheels will be having lunch with the astronauts next week. Maybe he can pick up a fuel cell at the nearest space center.

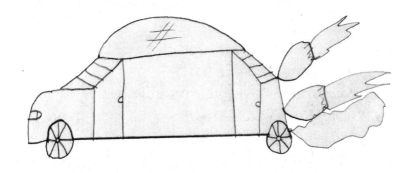

🐾 🐾 🐾 🐾 🐾 🐾 🐾

See the fuel cells with Dr. GreenWheels on page 181

Rainbow turns bright, daisy yellow. She's really proud of her cousin! Prius is the coolest car you've ever seen. He looks like he's made from real silver! He sparkles right in front of your eyes.

"Welcome to ThermaSip Village," Prius says softly.

Prius' house looks like a castle in the middle of the forest. It's painted leaf green to fit in with all the trees.

Everyone is really excited to see Prius. He's famous for being the fastest HyBrid on earth.

"We want you to race in the Bone Challenge Car Race," Dr. GreenWheels explains.

"You can win!" Rainbow beeps.

"Yeah," Coco and The Giz bark.

Prius is very quiet. "No," he says quietly.

"Why?" Dr. GreenWheels roars. "With your hybrid synergy drive, you can win without a problem!"

"Let me tell you about my synergy drive," Prius says kindly. "It's the best in the world. I run on gas and electricity. I recharge my own battery without even plugging into an electric outlet. However, I still need some gasoline. Since the Bone Challenge lasts two days, thirty minutes, and twenty seconds, I would need a few pit stops to refuel. Right now, I don't have any pit stops. How can I race without them?"

Which way do you go?

🐾 🐾 🐾 🐾 🐾 🐾 🐾

Build the pit stops and get Prius into the race on page 140
Tour ThermaSip and Bone Tree Forest on page 145

You, Coco, and The Giz climb into Shredder. Dr. GreenWheels honks unhappily, but he doesn't try to stop you.

Inside, Shredder looks like any normal car. He has dark blue seats and a dashboard like the cars from your neighborhood.

"Where are we going?" you ask.

"See the large button on the dashboard that says TIME?" Shredder replies. "Push it." You reach out to push the TIME button. You barely hear Shredder add quietly, "I'm a time machine."

Race back in time on the next page

Suddenly, everything changes around you.

"Get out," Shredder says. "Take a look around."

You, Coco, and The Giz slowly climb out of Shredder. You take a deep breath. Coco whimpers. The Giz growls. You're in a very scary place.

All around you is a big, smelly swamp. Giant trees are everywhere. Plants are higher than one hundred feet tall. It's hot, damp, and very hard to walk. Something seems to be moving toward your feet.

"Watch out for the meat-eating tetrapod!" Shredder yells.

You stare as a seven foot, slimy lizard crawls closer. From the corner of your eye, you see Coco and The Giz leap behind a tree.

Quickly, you jump out of the way, landing right next to the tree. When you look down near your feet, you see four large paws, four little paws, and something awful slithering between the trees. It looks like a six-foot long caterpillar with a zillion legs.

"Where are we?" you cry, shaking with fear.

As a hairy, black spider, bigger than Coco, walks by, Shredder hollers.

"Watch out for that spider," Shredder warns. "We're way back in time!" Shredder looks really weird in the swamp. Everyone knows that cars don't belong way back in time.

"This is hundreds of millions of years ago - long before the dinosaurs. It's called The Carboniferous Period."

You can't imagine what all this has to do with getting gas for the Bone Challenge.

"When all these trees, plants and water critters died," Shredder continues, "they sank to the bottom of the swamp. Over millions of years, they were buried under dirt, water, and rock. All that pressure and change in the earth made big pockets. The stuff in the pockets turned into oil."

Now you get it! Oil is called a fossil fuel because it took millions of years - and monster insects, plants, and tiny water critters - to make it.

"Oil is non-renewable," Shredder grumbles. "Once we use it up, it's gone. We can't make any more."

"What does oil have to do with gas for the race?" you ask.

"Oil is pumped up from the ground," Shredder explains. "Then it's made into a lot of different things like plastic, clothes, and toothbrushes. Most of it is used to make gasoline for airplanes, trucks, and buses."

". . . and cars," you add.

Before you can finish, Shredder interrupts.

You freeze.

"Duck!" Shredder yells.

A two-foot dragonfly, longer than your arm, flies right over your head. Thin, sticky wings brush against your face. You scream!

Coco and The Giz snap at the flying bug.

"Look down at the ground slowly," Shredder says, "so it doesn't see you."

"Let's get in the car!" you shout.

You don't want to wait around to see if you are to become dinner for a dragonfly.

Turn to the next page ➤

Race ahead to page 182

Principal CeeKay pushes a flashing button on her glasses. A bolt of electricity explodes across the room. The weirdest wizard you've ever seen appears in front of you.

"Meet E-Wiz," Principal CeeKay says.

E-Wiz wears a pointed hat with gold stars. His wand looks like a cell phone. You blink your eyes. E-Wiz looks totally different.

"Hmmmmm," E-Wiz hums. "I'm a transformer techie wizard. I look anyway you want . . . like a computer game."

"How can a transformer techie wizard help Toxic Town?" you ask.

E-Wiz shifts shape. "Let me show you. All you have to do is hold hands."

Everyone holds hands except Coco and The Giz. They hold paws.

E-Wiz taps your shoulder with his wand. Now the wand looks like a purple light stick.

☙ ☙ ☙ ☙ ☙ ☙ ☙

Go to the other side of the world on page 147
Stick to Toxic Town on page 148

Principal CeeKay pushes a button on her glasses. Suddenly the coolest wizard in the world is right in front of you.

"Yo, dude," Wizard Luna says.

Principal CeeKay high-fives the wizard.

"We need your help," you say.

Wizard Luna grins. "Don't I know that?" he laughs. "Toxic Town is nasty."

"It's going to close!" Bob cries.

Wizard Luna nods. "No kidding, man. This place needs a mean bath."

Coco yaps.

"Yo, Coco-nutty," Wizard Luna high-fives her.

You wonder how Wizard Luna knows Coco's nickname. He must really get around.

"What can the kids do to clean up Toxic Town?" Principal CeeKay asks.

"Mmmmmm," Wizard Luna rubs his beard.

Everyone waits quietly.

"I got it," Wizard Luna yells. He leaps in the air, does a

quick fly-around, and lands right in front of you.

This guy is crazier than a superhero-in-training, you think.

"Change the name!" Wizard Luna flips backwards three times and lands on his head. "Call it Non-Toxic Town," he adds, balancing on his pointed hat.

"Great idea," The Giz barks.

"I . . . like this . . . dog," Wizard Luna sings, flipping back to his feet.

"We need to do more than change the name," Daisy cries.

"Ahhhhh, my flower child," Wizard Luna sniffs the air. "Of course, you need to do more. You need to make Toxic Town non-toxic."

"How?" you demand.

Wizard Luna speaks in a whisper. "Some people call it the Luna Bulb. Others say it's Clean 9000. I kind of like Billy Bulb. It has that movie feel to it, know what I mean?"

You get ready to write one of the greatest stories in your life!

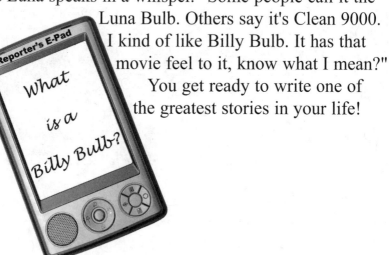

Reporter's E-Pad

What is a Billy Bulb?

Meet Billy Bulb on the next page ➡

"What's a Billy Bulb?" Principal CeeKay asks.

The words come out in bubbles from the wizard's mouth. "Crazy, bright, shiny, clean . . . magictastic."

"Magictastic?" You repeat.

"Yes," Wizard Luna shouts. "Billy Bulb is a magictastic light bulb that cleans up the mess! Replace the old incandescent light bulbs that everyone uses with Billy Bulbs and Toxic Town becomes Non-Toxic Town overnight!"

"How?" Daisy asks.

"It's simple." Wizard Luna says. "If every home in America changes just one light bulb to a Billy Bulb, we'd save enough energy to light over two million homes for a year. That means less electricity and less pollution. Just one Billy Bulb in every house would be like getting rid of the pollution from nearly 800,000 cars!"

"Think about what it would do in Toxic Town!" you shout.

Wizard Luna dances across the floor, spins in the air, and lands on his tippy toes. "A lot of people call Billy Bulb a compact fluorescent bulb. It lasts for years and saves people money."

"Wow," Coco yaps.

"There's a problem," Wizard Luna stops his dance. "You have to get people to use Billy Bulbs."

"The kids need to take action," Principal CeeKay cries.

"I have an idea!" you shout. "Why don't we have a contest? Everybody joins a school group. The group that gets the most people to change to Billy Bulbs wins."

"What do they win?" Principal CeeKay asks.

Wizard Luna chuckles. "That's easy. The winner gets my special wizard surprise goodie bag! There's no other one like it in the whole world."

Which group do you join?

🐾 🐾 🐾 🐾 🐾 🐾 🐾

The Bully Billy Bulbs on page 151
The Poster Artists on page 152
The Do-It-Yourselfers on page 156

Principal CeeKay grins. She pushes a button on her glasses. Suddenly, the yummiest wizard in the world is standing in front of you.

"Meet Eco-Nick," Principal CeeKay says.

Eco-Nick wears a chocolate wizard hat, holds a red licorice stick for a wand, and smells like cupcakes that popped right out of the oven.

"How can I help you?" Eco-Nick asks sweetly.

"How about some double turkey chip cookies?" Coco yelps.

"Toxic Town is in trouble," Principal CeeKay explains, ignoring Coco. "We need to clean it up."

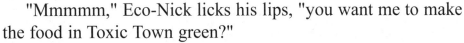

"Mmmmm," Eco-Nick licks his lips, "you want me to make the food in Toxic Town green?"

"Anyone want a green brush?" Coco yaps and leaps into the air with a mouthful of paintbrushes.

"Do we have to paint all of our food green?" Daisy asks.

"Let me show you," Eco-Nick blows a green, chewing gum bubble. He leads everyone into the school lunchroom. He points his licorice stick wand at a table, and suddenly there's a pile of delicious Big Macs. Everyone dives in for a bite!

"The burgers are great," you say, "but they're not green."

"Oh yes they are!" Eco-Nick takes a bite of red licorice from his wand. "A lot of hamburgers come from beef raised in rainforests, where all the trees and plants have been cut down. It's very bad for the

earth to lose her rainforests. Big Macs come from beef raised in fields that make the earth happy - never rainforests!"

"Wow!" you stare at your burger.

"Try this!" Eco-Nick chuckles as he waves his red licorice wand. You hardly notice the teeth marks in the candy.

There's a huge pumpkin pie on the table.

"Pumpkin pie isn't green," you say.

"No," Eco-Nick simmers. "Pumpkins are orange. This pumpkin pie is "green" because it comes from the Garden of

Eve Farm outside of town. The pumpkins are organic - grown without any nasty chemicals that are bad for people and the earth. Since the pumpkins are grown nearby, it takes fewer trucks to drive them to your table. Fewer trucks on the roads mean less pollution in the air."

"If everyone eats green food, can we help clean up Toxic Town?" you ask.

"Yes!" Eco-Nick bubbles happily.

Suddenly, lightning and thunder flash through the lunchroom. Your heart pounds in fear. A wizard, who looks like twisted spaghetti, appears out of thin air. You look at the awful words on his hat.

Down With Green

"I won't let Toxic Town food go green," the Twisted Spaghetti Wizard roars. He raises his wand and Eco-Nick disappears.

Now everyone knows that a Twisted Spaghetti Wizard is no

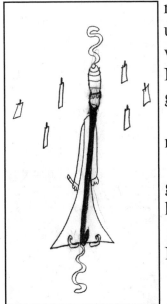

match for a superhero dog team. The Giz uses his Meat Vision to change the wizard into a pile of moldy meatballs. Next, Coco uses her Sanitizing Breath to get rid of the mess.

"He's gone," you cry. "Now we can make Toxic Town food green."

You look around, but Eco-Nick is gone! The only thing left of the wizard is his half-eaten licorice stick wand.

"We can't do anything without Eco-Nick," Daisy cries.

"We'll find him," you say.

Which way do you go?

🐾 🐾 🐾 🐾 🐾 🐾 🐾

Look for Eco-Nick in the principal's office on page 158
Search for Eco-Nick on Factory Street on page 159
Hunt for Eco-Nick on the farm on page 160

The students in Parliament Place School, Long Island, New York asked their community to go green. They sent out 200 cards that read:

Coco and The Giz Go Green

This year at Parliament Place School we're going green to make the earth a better place. I made this card for you from reused and recycled materials.

Parliament Place School is doing a lot of green things. Please help us save the earth! Do something to go green and tell us about it on the enclosed postcard.

I'll share your ideas with my classmates in school and on our website. We'll show everyone how people in our community are going green too!

NEWSDAY, our Long Island newspaper, chose us to be part of their community service program, **FutureCorps.**

We got a lot of postcards from people in our community!

I go green by taking mass transit wherever I go. When I drive, I always travel with someone else. - Nick

I planted two new trees this fall and recycled my worn clothes for others. - Norann

I go green with Mr. Luna's Bright Idea *to use compact fluorescent light bulbs.* - James

We always use recycled paper at our bank.. - Lynette

I recycle and ride a bike. - Donald

I grow a vegetable garden. It's really green. - Eileen

Meet the first graders in the project on page 112
Meet the kindergarteners in the project on page 79
See what our State Assemblyman told us on page 167

Coco and The Giz thank the first grade Which Way student-authors

Alexander Iacono
Alexandra Sulca Leonardo
Alexandra Caruso
Amanda Zwiebel
Amanda Brady
Andrew Becvar
Anthony Neri
Aniya Smith
Ariyanna Walston
Bryan Martinez
Cameron Charles
Cassidy Crutchley
Cecilia Ali
Chelsea Thomas
Christina Green
Christopher Ramsay
Clyde Williams
Connor Avolin
Dale Angelo Malusay
David Catapano

Delicia James
Diana Wooley
Donovan Sibblies
Edelyne Cine
Emily Valensky
Emily Thiele
Evelyn Valles
Franck Aly Montour
Frank Maguire
Freddy Obando
Gabriel Zimmer
Gabriella Borgo
Gina Liantonio
Haley Dennerlein
Hallie Bones
Haris Mansoor
Jacob Altman
Jason Lella
Jason Guillen
Javier Guzman Portillo
Jordan Bux
Jordan Barker
Joseph Romano
Jose Sanchez
Julia Stanger
Kaila Jean-Charles
Katherine Lopez
Kayla Kelly
Kayla Schneider
Kayla Mahr

Logan Johns
Maham Baig
Maria Khan
Marissa Demetriou
Matthew Klages
Michael Perez
Michael Quinn
Mikayla Pariseau
Nicholas DeStafano
Nicholas Jordan
Nicola Calabrese
Nicole Ruiz Torres
Nicole Zacarias
Quadir Russell
Richard Bellino
Robert Baker
Samantha Howe
Samantha Rodriguez
Saraswati Dubay
Schuyler Valensky
Sohail Ahmed
Thomas Carter
Thriston Briscoe
Tifany Ayala
Tiffany Decker
Trevor Daly
Tyler Small
William Muller
Zachary Pulis

Officer George leads you, Parliament Cat, Coco and The Giz off the purple skateboard and down steps made from old telephone books.

"Follow me," Officer George says, "to see how garbage critters can make the earth happy."

You, Parliament Cat, Coco, and The Giz follow Officer George.

"Look," Officer George points.

Right in the middle of the landfill is a large power plant! It's surrounded by garbage critters, eating everything in sight! When the critters finish eating, they go to a big pipe on top of the factory and burp in the landfill gas.

"The garbage critters burp the landfill gas into the power plant," Officer George explains. "Then the power plant turns it into electricity."

"Wow!" The Giz barks. "The landfill gases don't get the chance to pollute the air and make global warming worse."

"You got it!" Officer George says. "A landfill gas power plant uses the gas to make energy that we can use," Officer George adds. "Power plants like this, make enough electricity for millions of homes."

"Electricity to keep my beef fudge ice cream frozen, cook my chicken mush, and run my TV!" Coco yaps.

"Right," Officer George grins. "It gives us electricity, puts the garbage critters to work, and shrinks the landfill. Everyone wins."

What a story for *Book Web*. You can see the headlines now.

REPORTER DISCOVERS GOOD IN GARBAGE CRITTERS

All you need is a great photo and your story is done.

🐾 🐾 🐾 🐾 🐾 🐾 🐾

Take your photo on page 162

How many things
do you recognize?

Find the Happy Meal bag, the French fry container,
the carryout bags, the tray, and the napkins. All of these
items are made from recycled paper and cardboard.
McDonald's spends more than $100 million each year
to buy recycled paper and cardboard
to keep our earth cleaner.

You, Parliament Cat, Coco, and The Giz leap off the purple skateboard. You slide down a mountain of trash and face Officer George.

"Follow me," Officer George says. "There are globs of yucky gunk here in this part of the landfill."

The smell is really bad and slimy, muddy stuff oozes over your shoes.

"Where are we going?" you ask.

"Look," Officer George says.

Right in the middle of the landfill is a building.

"It's a biodiesel plant," Officer George says.

"Does that kind of plant grow cherries?" Coco asks.

"That kind of plant is a factory. It doesn't make anything that you can eat, but cars and trucks can use it," Officer George answers.

"What's biodiesel?" you ask.

"Biodiesel is a fuel for cars and trucks that is made from organic stuff like plants and cooking oil."

"Cool," Parliament Cat meows.

You think about the garbage people throw out everyday. There are the green peas you didn't eat for dinner and the moldy bread you hid behind the TV. There's the poop from the kitty litter, the grass from mowing the lawn, and dead leaves from the backyard. It's all the biomass that the garbage critters eat for dinner!

Officer George reads your mind. "The garbage critters spit their biomass dinner into the building," Officer George explains. "All that rotten food, from our homes, farms, and cities is biomass. When the garbage critters spit it into the landfill biodiesel plant, it turns into fuel for cars and trucks."

". . . and school buses," you add.

The garbage critters are helping the earth!

It's a great story! You can see the headlines now.

BOOK WEB REPORTER LEARNS
FROM GARBAGE CRITTERS

All you need is a good photo and your story will be done.

🐾 🐾 🐾 🐾 🐾 🐾

Take your photo on page 164

Thank you McDonald's

Coco and The Giz thank our special support
team from the North Babylon Schools

Dave Casamento, Director of Science

**Ken Luna, Science Teacher,
Robert Moses Middle School**

**Jim Haley, Coordinator
of Business and Technology**

Monica Cruz, art student

Everything is inky black. You hear strange noises, but you can't see anything. You think about the houses that have no lights and the cities that waste so much electricity.

You even think about Coco's two-inch-high, mini tornado.

What's going on? The Willow Pet Hotel doesn't waste power. It uses solar power from the roof. Why should the lights go out?

Suddenly, you hear a voice. It's Dr. GreenWheels. He's very cranky. "Where's the dumb human?" he hollers.

You run outside. Coco and The Giz wave to you from the sunroof. Dr. GreenWheels grinds his gears. You jump in the car. It smells just like Annie's Mac & Cheese. The Giz must have been pushing the green snack buttons again . . .

"You sure took your time," Dr. GreenWheels mutters as he takes off. "What are the Dirty Energy Creeps doing in a place like this?" you cry.

Solve the mystery on the next page. ➡️

"You don't know much about Dirty Energy Creeps," The Giz woofs.

Coco leaps on you. She gives you a sticky, face wash with her tongue. You would rather use soap than Coco's tongue to clean your face.

The Giz sighs. "Dirty Energy Creeps will do anything to get rid of clean electricity," he explains.

Clean electricity is green power. It's made from things that make the earth happy, like wind, water, and sun. Some people call it renewable energy because it doesn't get used up.

Dirty Energy Creeps want electricity that's made from yucky stuff like coal and oil. Some people call it non-renewable energy because it gets used up. Once the coal and oil are gone, there will be nothing left to make electricity. When people use clean energy, they never run out of sunlight, water, and wind!

Dr. GreenWheels flies to the roof of The Willow Pet Hotel.

The Dirty Energy Creeps are destroying Mr. Marc's solar power panels on the roof. You, Coco, and The Giz leap out, as Dr.GreenWheels shines his green beam on the closest Dirty Energy Creep.

The Dirty Energy Creep freezes. He can't run, but he can still use his remote control to shoot chunks of bubble gum on the solar power panels. Another creep, with rainbow teeth, does a scratch attack with his evil purple claws. A tiny gnome-creep cuts through the wires with his pointy red hat.

The roof is crawling with hundreds of Dirty Energy Creeps! There aren't enough green beams to freeze them all.

"What can we do?" You cry.

You, Coco, and The Giz put your heads together.

"I can use my Meat Vision and turn them into hamburgers," The Giz suggests.

"All that meat could break the solar power panels," you say.

"I'll use my Amazing Tail Zap," Coco yelps.

"Uh . . . I think you need some more practice with that," you say kindly.

"I got it!" The Giz barks. "We can make our tails 20 feet long and whack them out of there!"

All of a sudden, Coco leaps into the air. After all, she is a superhero-in-training. She opens her mouth and blows out her Sanitizing Breath. Coco is pretty good with that superpower.

The Dirty Energy Creeps scream, sending shivers down your back. Before you know it they're . . . clean!

Everyone knows that a clean Dirty Energy Creep is useless.

You and The Giz cheer as Coco shoots her Sanitizing Breath on the solar power panels. The bubble gum, scratches, and dirt melt away!

Mr. Marc climbs onto the roof. "You saved the Willow Pet Hotel!" he shouts. "Our solar power panels can continue to make us clean energy," he says as the lights go back on.

Everything goes back to normal. The cats, in cool tee shirts, play their video games. The poodle dries her pink fur. The dogs strum their electric guitars and howl. It sounds really good. Best of all, you have a great story for *Book Web News*!

❀ ❀ ❀ ❀ ❀ ❀ ❀

Pick up a photo for your story about solar panels on page 168

"Mr. Marc," you cry. "Where are you?"

Everything is inky black. You're afraid to move and bump into an evil Dirty Energy Creep. What can you do?

You think of the things you can do without electricity. If it's during the day, you can go outside, play hide-and-seek, soccer, or ride your bike. Coco and The Giz can play Frisbee and tug-of-war. Coco can practice her Amazing Tail Zap. Of course, superheroes wouldn't mind eating up all the yummy ice cream before it melts at The Willow Pet Hotel.

What can you do at night without electricity? There are radio and hand-held video games. The dogs with electric guitars can sing, and the cats can sleep on the couch. Coco and The Giz can tell scary stories and play Super Sniffer with their noses.

You can even play board games with a flashlight.

Suddenly, you hear Mr. Marc's voice.

"Are you OK?" he asks.

"Yes," you say. "There are really a lot of things you can do without electricity."

"Right!" Mr. Marc says happily. "That's the whole point. If we did more of those things, we would save a lot of electricity."

You know that it's very important to save electricity. It makes the earth healthier.

"What about The Dirty Energy Creeps?" You ask, your voice shaking.

Mr. Marc laughs. "Oh, that was just a trick!" He flips a switch and the electricity is back. "Dirty Energy Creeps love all the dirt and soot that comes from coal. Our solar panels get energy from the sun. Our solar energy keeps it too clean for those creeps!

You grab your reporter's e-pad. "Where do they go?"

Mr. Marc frowns. "They have a lot of places to go because there's a lot of dirty energy being made all the time."

Save electricity with the Keyspan Kids on page 169
See real solar panels on page 168
Track more Dirty Energy Creeps on page 87

It's really dark. You feel your way around The Willow Pet Hotel until you find the kitchen. It's hard to find anything when there are no lights. Finally you touch the freezer. You open the door. It's not cold anymore.

Freezers need electricity. The Dirty Energy Creeps have turned off the power! Lots of beef swirl ice cream drips on your sneakers. You bend down to clean up the mess, but end up covered in mucky, ice cream glop. The only thing you can do is take a nap. Gooey dreams to you!

The end of this dark adventure.

Coco and The Giz thank some very special humans who helped make our book possible

Cynthia Eichinger

Pat & Cliff Kase

You stare at the sign.

"Who is Ms. Fossil Face and why did they fire her?" you ask.

"Grrrrr," Coco sighs. The pink hat with red-hot sparkles is still in her mouth. Even a superhero-in-training can't talk with her mouth full.

The Giz takes over. "Ms. Fossil Face was once the most beautiful blob in the world. She had purple skin, green eyes, and big red lips."

You write some notes on your reporter's e-pad.

"It's very sad," The Giz continues. "Ms. Fossil Face ran the power plant. People needed more and more electricity to run stuff like refrigerators, computers, and televisions. She burned more coal to make them happy. Finally, she burned so much coal that her purple skin turned grimy gray, her big, red lips got dry and dirty, and she wasn't pretty anymore."

"She can use clean energy," you suggest.

"She wants to," The Giz frowns. "She has been learning about ways to make clean energy."

"Now that Ms. Fossil Face is fired, she'll never have the chance!" Coco yelps and spits red-hot sparkles.

"Let's find her," you cry. "You can use your Super Sniffer to search. Then she can get her job back."

"Great idea," The Giz barks happily.

The Giz uses his Super Sniffer to search the power plant. He starts at the piles of coal outside and moves to the boilers where the coal is burned. Too hot there! He follows the steam from the burning coal to the turbines and generators - the machines that make the electricity. No Ms. Fossil Face! The Giz searches the transformers, where electricity begins its trip down the wires to your school, the local McDonald's, and your computer at home.

"She's not there," The Giz says.

The Giz super sniffs the control room where there are buttons, lights, and screens everywhere. Then he checks out the offices and finally, the lunchroom.

"I found her!" The Giz cries.

You and Coco run to the lunchroom. It's empty and dark. The Giz found Ms. Fossil Face in the corner. You turn on the lights and cry, "We're here to save you."

Ms. Fossil Face is covered with goop, grease, and grime. Piles of mail surround her. There are open letters everywhere. She's crying, as tears of mud run down her blobs onto the envelopes.

🐾 🐾 🐾 🐾 🐾 🐾 🐾

Read Ms. Fossil Face's muddy letters on page 170
Build a windmill and help Ms. Fossil Face on page 172
See a plant that makes electricity from garbage on page 162

127

"Who is Ms. Fossil Face?" you ask.

"She was the most beautiful blob in the world!" The Giz says. "She had purple skin, green eyes, big, red lips and everyone loved her."

Coco tosses the pink hat with red-hot sparkles in the air and barks fiercely. She sounds more like a broken washing machine than a superhero-in-training.

"Ms. Fossil Face tried to make everyone happy," The Giz continues, ignoring Coco. "People used more and more  electricity. They wouldn't save or conserve energy. Ms. Fossil Face just burned more coal to please everyone. People wanted so much electricity that Ms. Fossil Face turned all gray and ugly with smoke and coal dust. She became the ugliest blob in the world!"

You write some notes on your reporter's e-pad.

"She really wants to get clean energy to make people and the earth happy," The Giz says. "Instead, The Dirty Energy Creeps have fired her!"

You tear down the sign.

"No way are The Dirty Energy Creeps firing Ms. Fossil Face," you cry.

Coco leaps into the air and practices her fierce bark. This time she sounds like a frog with a bad croak.

You open the door to the power plant. You, Coco, and The Giz go inside.

The power plant is crawling with Dirty Energy Creeps.

None of them look the same, and they all have different names. Your stomach does a flip flop.

Dr. Yuck faces you. He is a really tall Dirty Energy Creep. His nose is black and brown with bloody, red spots. He waves a long evil tail over his head.

Poop-man stands behind Dr. Yuck. Poop-man is slimy and wears a gold shirt, tucked into silver pants.

King Dirty Dragon has more wrinkles than you have ever seen in your life. Darkside, Evil Gnome, and Alien Jake are there too.

You're terrified! Are The Dirty Energy Creeps going to attack you?

"What do we do?" You whisper to Coco and The Giz.

Your voice shakes and your hands tremble.

"Get out of here," Dr. Yuck roars.

"Get out of here," the other Dirty Energy Creeps roar.

You know it's over. The Dirty Energy Creeps will fight you. There are hundreds of them and only three of you. You close your eyes and wait for the pain.

Suddenly, it gets very cold. You open your eyes. A green beam is freezing the Dirty Energy Creeps one-by-one. The place looks like a museum with hundreds of Dirty Energy Creep statues.

"Do you think I'd let these bullies pick on my Coco-nutty?" Dr. GreenWheels grumbles.

Coco drops the pink, pointy hat with red-hot sparkles.

"No!" you cry.

It's too late. Coco fires her Amazing Tail Zap at the frozen statues. Suddenly, it's raining Dirty Energy Creeps.

"You don't threaten superheroes," The Giz woofs.

You want to laugh, but the Dirty Energy Creeps are raining really hard. "What are you going to do with them now?" You gasp.

Coco and The Giz look at each other.

Out of nowhere, the ugliest blob with an open, pink umbrella floats down between the raining Dirty Energy Creeps.

"Ms. Fossil Face," The Giz cries. "You're safe."

Ms. Fossil Face smiles, but you see tears run down her face.

"Why don't you make them into Clean Energy Nerds, Coco?" Ms. Fossil Face whispers.

"Send them to the Hydro School," The Giz adds.

"Is that a school for statues?" You ask.

"No, it's a great place," Ms. Fossil Face giggles. She has the sweetest voice in the world! "The Hydro School is where you learn how to go green every day. You learn not to make garbage and how to recycle. You have to watch "The Environment Show" until you know how to make the earth healthy. Most importantly, you get to work at the Hydropower Plant, where you use water to make clean electricity.

"Wahoooooooo!" The Giz barks.

"Go for it, Coco-nutty," Dr. GreenWheels says.

"Once these Dirty Energy Creeps become Clean Energy Nerds at Hydro School, I'll be able to clean up the power plant," Ms. Fossil Face says happily.

Coco faces the frozen and raining Dirty Energy Creeps. She opens her mouth. You're not too worried because Coco is pretty good with her Sanitizing Breath.

With one single huff, Coco sends every Dirty Energy Creep at the power plant directly to Hydro School!

You, Ms. Fossil Face, Dr. GreenWheels, and The Giz cheer. It's a very special moment for a superhero-in-training!

❁ ❁ ❁ ❁ ❁ ❁ ❁

See real hydroelectric power in action on page 174

You, Coco, and The Giz run around the side of the building. You see an open door.

"Come on," you say, "we're going to shut down this power plant."

"Great idea," The Giz says.

The three of you go through the door. The control room is locked. The Giz uses his Super Strength to push open the doors.

Inside the control room there are buttons, lights, and screens everywhere. There's a big "on-off" switch. You rush to the switch and turn everything off.

The coal stops burning.

The machines stop making electricity.

The lights, refrigerators, computers, and televisions in houses all shut down.

You, Coco, and The Giz are in complete darkness.

The earth might be safer now, but no one has electricity.

Until you find a better way to make electricity, you get to stay in the dark!

The end of this dark adventure.

Where will I live when the rainforest is gone?
Stop cutting down the rainforests
before it's too late!

Ethie brakes at the sign that says "Corn Farm."

You, Coco, and The Giz jump out. You can't believe your eyes. All the corn is gone!

Coco races through the field and finds one, lonely ear of corn. She plops it on Ethie's hood. Ethie laughs sadly.

You read the words on a sign at the edge of the field.

Sold Out! All our corn was used for corn chips, popcorn, and tortillas. We have nothing left for ethanol! Come back next crop.

A single tear runs down Ethie's windshield.

"Don't worry," you say, "we'll find some ethanol by next year's race.

"I know what to do." Coco yelps, "Let's have some popcorn and watch a movie."

Everyone agrees that it's the end of this corny adventure.

Slurp ice cream on page 48
Save energy on page 157

Ethie speeds over to the sugar cane fields.

You, Coco, and The Giz jump out.

There are a zillion dogs and farmers standing in the field having a barbecue! The smell of hot dogs, hamburgers, and ribs makes you hungry. The Giz licks his lips.

You don't see any sugar cane.

"Where's the sugar cane?" You ask a farmer who has four hamburgers on his plate.

"It was a great season," the farmer says, ketchup dripping from his mouth. "We sold all our sugar to places that make things that kids love, like jellybeans, chocolate, and McFlurries . . . yum!"

Ethie honks sadly.

"You need some cheering up," the farmer continues. "How about all of you joining our farm barbecue?"

Coco leaps into the air and lands on Ethie. "Please let's go to the barbecue," she whimpers.

Ethie giggles "Let's go."

You and The Giz share a stack of hamburgers, but you know who gets most of them.

🐾 🐾 🐾 🐾 🐾 🐾 🐾

Race with the HyBrids on page 55
Hang out with the GasGuys on page 58

Ethie stops short in the landfill as she sees Oiler zoom in her direction.

Landfill is a fancy name for garbage dump. The Gizco Island Garbage Dump looks like all the other landfills around the world. Trash is everywhere - from soggy paper and plastic bottles to smelly yuck that makes your stomach do flip-flops.

Tears run down Ethie's windshield.

Coco dives like a nutty torpedo into a pile of rotting food. She retrieves a moldy, half-eaten corn-on-the-cob and plops it in front of Ethie. "Will this help?" Coco yaps.

Ethie watches as Oiler whips around the landfill. It's hard to keep him still. He drives in circles around her, sending torn, plastic supermarket bags in all directions.

"There's no fuel for me," Oiler bellows.

"The GreenWheels won't be in this year's race," Ethie wails.

"Wait!" You say. "There's a way and it's just around the corner.

You talk as Ethie, Oiler, Coco, and The Giz listen carefully.

"Everyone knows that ethanol comes from crops like corn and sugar cane. Do you know how it's made?"

"Sure," Ethie rumbles. "You ferment the corn and sugar."

"What's fermenting?" Oiler asks.

"Fermenting is when food changes into something else," The Giz barks. "It's like making grapes into wine, apples into cider, and milk into cheese."

"Right," you say. "Something has to make the food ferment. For example, you use happy little critters to make ethanol from corn."

"So?" Ethie revs her engine impatiently. "I can't race on happy little critters."

"Take a look around," you say gently. "Why are there birds in the landfill?"

"They're eating," Coco yaps.

"Right!" You grin. "Birds love to eat stuff like old food scraps, moldy bread, and seeds."

"Yuck," Coco yelps.

Between the plastic bottles and soggy paper in the landfill, there are piles of other stuff. There's the poop from the kitty litter, rotten food from the store, old lawn clippings, and dead leaves. There's broken wood furniture, corn stalks left over from the fields, string beans the kids didn't eat for dinner, and everything restaurants and supermarkets throw out.

"That's biomass," The Giz says. "Biomass is organic stuff - or anything that comes from living things."

"Ethanol comes from living things," Ethie says.

"The oil I use for my fuel comes from living things too!" Oiler roars.

"Right!" You shout. "We have all this biomass in the landfill that no one wants!"

Gear up with biomass on the next page.

You, Coco, and The Giz hop into Ethie's car. Oiler follows you.

"Let's go to the waste-to-energy plant," you say.

"What's that?" Ethie asks.

"It's where they turn biomass from the landfill into fuel," you explain.

In minutes, you're in front of a big building.

"That's where they turn the garbage into ethanol," you say.

"Will there be enough for the race?" Ethie asks.

"There will be enough biomass for both you and Oiler," you grin.

"I have an idea," Coco woofs happily, "I'll use my Amazing Tail Zap to speed up the plant and get enough ethanol and oil for ten Bone Challenges!"

"No!" everyone cries.

Coco doesn't listen. You close your eyes as she fires her Amazing Tail Zap. You expect to see a giant chocolate crunch dinosaur or a smelly, electric sneaker instead of the plant.

You're wrong.

This time, Coco gets it right.

🐾 🐾 🐾 🐾 🐾 🐾 🐾

Ride the Bone Challenge fast lane with Ethie on page 176
Hit the Bone Challenge track with Oiler on page 180
Pump in the garbage on page 164

Tri-State Biodiesel collects used cooking oil from New York City restaurants. The oil is recycled into biodiesel fuel.

Compliments of Tri-State Biodiesel, LLC
New York, NY

"The fuel of the future . . . today."

No one knows what to do.

HyBrids are very kind, so Prius says nothing. Rainbow turns gray-blue, and Dr. GreenWheels tries to make her feel better. Coco and The Giz stare at the Bone Trees.

It's up to you to figure out how Prius can race. The Bone Challenge starts tomorrow so there's not much time.

You look at Coco and The Giz.

"Can a superhero dog build a HyBrid pit stop?" You ask.

"I have my Amazing Tail Zap," Coco says hopefully.

"Sure," The Giz says, "you'll try to build a pit stop and end up with a peach pit."

"Don't pick on me," Coco whimpers.

"Take it easy, Coco-nutty," Dr. GreenWheels says. "We'll figure something out."

"Let's think," you mumble. "A pit stop is the place where cars refuel and make repairs during a race."

Everyone is very quiet.

"A pit stop for Prius needs gas," you continue. "The Giz can use his Super Strength to bring in the gas."

"That's a great idea," Prius agrees. "I also need some special motor oil to run smoothly . . . just like a GasGuy."

"Easy," you say happily. "The Giz's Super Strength can bring in the gasoline and motor oil. Coco's Amazing Zap can turn a bucket of bones from the Bone Trees into spare tires."

Prius is very quiet. "It could work," he says softly.

Everyone looks at Coco.

"I'll try really hard," she whimpers.

You grab a bucket from Prius' backyard and run into Bone Tree Forest. It doesn't take you long to fill it with bones. You run back and put the bucket down right in front of Coco.

"Practice," you say. "We need spare tires."

You hold your breath.

"Think," The Giz nudges Coco.

"You can do it, Coco-nutty," Dr. GreenWheels honks.

Coco faces the bucket of bones. She takes a deep breath and fires her Amazing Tail Zap.

The bucket of bones turns into . . . a pile of rubber toilet paper.

"No!" Coco wails.

"You can do it," The Giz says. "Try harder."

Coco closes her eyes, crosses her paws, and fires another Amazing Tail Zap. There's pink smoke everywhere! Your eyes burn as you wait for it to clear. It smells just like watermelon lollipops.

"Sorry," Coco whimpers.

"Wait!" Rainbow shouts. She's the color of the sun - so bright that you need sunglasses to look at her.

Beneath all the pink smoke is a pile of rubber tires!

Dr. GreenWheels honks loudly. You're not sure if he's honking for Prius, Rainbow or Coco!

"We're headed for the Bone Challenge," you shout.

Coco flips high into the air. The superhero-in-training saves the day.

It's the race of your life on the next page.

Prius is ready to go! His synergy drive is all revved up. He sparkles like diamonds in the sun. Coco and The Giz set up all the pit stops. Now it's time to win the race.

Hundreds of cars line up for the race. A huge crowd of people, dogs, and cars cheer loudly. The air is filled with excitement.

Prius' engine is so quiet that you hardly know it's running. "Would you like to ride with me?" He asks gently.

You can't believe your ears. Prius wants you to ride with him in the Bone Challenge. You're the guest of the greatest HyBrid on the planet! You grab your reporter's e-pad, jump into the front seat, put on your helmet, and snap on the seatbelt.

Inside, Prius is made of very soft leather. There are buttons, dials, and lights all over the dashboard. It's the quietest car you've ever heard -electricity doesn't make noise like other cars. The next two days, thirty minutes, and twenty seconds of your life will go very fast.

A big dog with floppy purple ears holds a green racing flag at the starting line. Suddenly, everyone is quiet. You hold your breath. The green flag is up.

You're off! The Annual Bone Challenge begins.

There's so much to see. Prius races down Gizco Island Roads, plunges into the ocean, and flies in the sky, keeping ahead of all the other cars. It's the most amazing race ever.

You watch schools of bright purple fish swim outside your window as Prius skims the ocean floor. When he hits the air, a flock of seagulls moves aside. They're no match for synergy drive! As you circle the volcano, a blue car flips off the edge and drops out of the race. Another car bumps into a Bone Tree, rolls over, and hits the road again. A strange-looking orange car does a loop-de-loop in the sky. You can't believe what

you're seeing! Coco and The Giz work the pit stops. Rainbow cheers you on. The sun rises and sets twice. Your reporter's e-pad is bursting with notes.

Finally, there are twenty seconds to go! Prius is in the lead, followed by two other cars. All of you are bumper-to-bumper. Your heart pounds wildly.

Suddenly, Prius becomes a superstar! He shifts into high synergy drive and sizzles like the hottest star in the galaxy.

"Go!" You scream at the top of your lungs.

Prius zips ahead by a headlight.

The other cars are so close! The black-and-white checkered winner's flag is right in front of your eyes. Can Prius make it?

Without warning you hear a loud, awful sound. There are

honks, barks and engines roaring. People are screaming. You know what it is. It's the sound of the Gizco Island cheer.

Prius edges forward. The other cars stay with him. Suddenly they're a bumper behind. You scream so loud that you lose your voice. Rainbow snuggles next to Dr. GreenWheels on the sidelines. Coco and The Giz are barking like crazy.

Prius races past the checkered flag!

Prius HyBrid wins the Bone Challenge!

There's a rainstorm of chocolate covered raisins as the crowd celebrates. Prius zooms through the candy, his silver skin gleaming.

Everyone honks Prius' name.

Prius glides into the winner's circle to get his prize.

You jump out to hug Coco. "Great, Coco-nutty," you shout.

Coco opens her mouth to lick you and a roll of rubber toilet paper lands in your lap.

"Sorry about that," Coco yelps.

Check out the real Prius on page 212

It's a great day in ThermaSip Village. You jump onto Prius' buttery soft leather seat and follow Rainbow. She turns a tasty cotton candy pink as she leads you on a tour through Bone Tree Forest. The dogs and puppies follow you everywhere. You open the window and grab a bone from the nearest tree. You take a bite and discover that it's really for the dogs. You'd rather be eating ice cream.

Prius is happy to miss the Bone Challenge for a wonderful day with friends and family in Bone Tree Forest. You love every minute of the ride.

The end of this gentle adventure.

Coco and The Giz thank our gold and silver
sponsors who helped make this book possible

Atlantic Toyota
Cartridge World U.S.A.
Central Business Systems
Nick LaRocco
JohnsonDiversey
Keyspan Energy
McDonald's
ThermaSIP
The Willow Pet Hotel

Compliments of the Basel Action Network, 2006

It seems as though that purple light stick put you at a place that smells worse than Toxic Town. The air is filled with white smoke and it's hard to breathe. Some kids cough. You're surrounded by piles of black plastic. You shiver. The piles line the street, surround the houses, and spill into the river.

"Where are we?" you choke.

"On the other side of the world," E-Wiz says, "in a very poor country."

"What's that?" you say pointing to a pile of black plastic.

A little boy jumps onto one of the yucky piles. He's playing.

"No!" Coco cries.

"Stop!" The Giz barks.

The kids wave at the little boy. Everyone knows that playing in the mucky plastic can make him sick.

"How can we help him?" you shout.

🐾 🐾 🐾 🐾 🐾 🐾 🐾

Jump in the yucky pile to save the little boy on page 184
Get help from E-Wiz on page 185

E-Wiz's purple light stick zaps you into Toxic Town Library. The kids, Coco, and The Giz crowd around Chief Dave at his computer.

Suddenly E-Wiz pops out of Chief Dave's computer. He looks like a character from your favorite book.

"What do books have to do with cleaning up Toxic Town?" you ask.

"Ahhhh," E-Wiz says, zooming around the bookshelves and magazine racks. "Paper," he howls.

Of course! Books are made from paper. Each year, in the United States alone, paper is used to make over 2 billion books, 350 million magazines, and 24 billion newspapers.

E-Wiz reads your mind. He hovers like a helicopter over your head. "Right!" he booms. "We use over 1 million tons of paper to make books each year. That's about the same weight as ten million sixth graders."

"Wow," you whisper, as you write the facts on your reporter's e-pad.

"Does that mean we should stop reading books?" Coco yaps.

"NO!" E-Wiz dives into the library's book bin. Books fly in

every direction. E-Wiz looks like a red electric guitar when he comes up for air.

"Books are very important. All you have to do is change the paper in books," E-Wiz says, "and that will make the earth very happy."

"Why does the earth care?" Daisy asks.

"Paper, my lovely," E-Wiz squeals. "Most paper comes from trees in the forest. Trees give off oxygen, the stuff that people, dogs, and wizards need to breathe. The trees soak up carbon dioxide, the stuff that people, dogs, and wizards breathe *out*. It's a great system. Trees keep the earth very healthy . . . unless people cut them down. We use about 500,000 trees just to print the Sunday newspaper!"

"That's 26 million trees per year," The Giz growls.

"How do we get paper without cutting down all those trees?" Bob asks."

"Meet my buddies," E-Wiz screeches like a bad microphone.

Who do you want to meet?

🐾 🐾 🐾 🐾 🐾 🐾 🐾

T-shore the tree kid on page 187
Espresso Book Machine on page 192

Coco and The Giz thank our community
sponsors for helping us go green

**Applebee's
Astro Masonry & Supply Company
Deer Park Bowl, Ltd.
Pet Supplies Plus
Peter Lombardo, Licensed Electrician
The Beacon
The Home Depot**

The Bully Billy Bulbs are really tough. They yell and force people to listen to them.

Everyone knows you can't bully people into changing light bulbs.

Have fun with all the Toxic Town bullies!

The end of this useless adventure.

The Poster Artists draw and paint colorful posters. They rush over to Central Business Systems to get lots of copies of their posters from the best machines.

The posters are in black and white, bright colors, and some have great photos. Best of all, they have a lot to say. Some of the words are funny, others are serious. They tell people how great it is to use Billy Bulbs.

Central Business Systems helps them hang posters everywhere. They're a big success!

Check out more cool posters on the next page

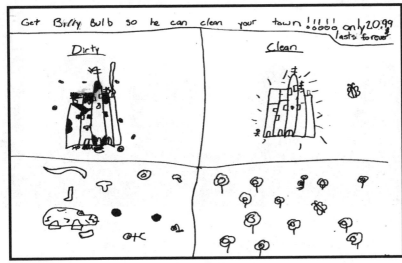

The do-it-yourselfers know that the best way to spread a good idea is to do it. They put Billy Bulbs in their homes. They tell all their friends and family to put Billy Bulbs in *their* homes. Suddenly, it's like the latest toy. Every family in Toxic Town has to have at least one Billy Bulb in their house.

Before you know it, Toxic Town has become Non-Toxic Town. Everyone is really happy! Wizard Luna hands you his special surprise goodie bag. You grab the huge, velvet bag and reach deep inside. You feel a lot of different shapes. One by one you pick each out.

You get all the Sticky Bubble Chews, Jumping Chocolate Caterpillars, and Sour Powers you can eat for your whole life.

You get a note for "no homework ever again."

You get all the dog treats that Coco and The Giz can eat for their whole lives.

You get to write about Billy Bulbs. Your story will be printed in a world famous newspaper, *The Beacon*.

The last thing you get is a Billy Bulb for every kid in the world!

Check out the real *Luna's Bright Idea* on page 194

KEYSPAN helps YOU and the Earth!

You can save energy now!
Find the compact fluorescent light bulb and use it.
Find the light switch, and turn it off.
Find the baby oak tree, and plant one at home.
Find the bicycle, and pedal instead of drive.

🐾 🐾 🐾 🐾 🐾 🐾 🐾

Search for a new principal on page 62

Everyone runs to Principal CeeKay's new office.

You peek in. On the walls there are lots of Toxic Town drawings by the kids.

You open the closets and all the drawers, but only find more artwork. There's no place for a wizard to hide here.

🐾 🐾 🐾 🐾 🐾 🐾 🐾

Visit the real Principal CeeKay in her office on page 197

Eco-Nick may have gone this way, so Coco and The Giz sniff along the path to Factory Street. You and the kids from Toxic Town follow the superheroes. Everyone says that candy factories are here, but you find only a street filled with litter. The air is gray with smoke and fumes. Sludge bubbles out of the sewers.

You wonder how candy can come from this street.

Just the thought of it makes you shiver. You still must find the sweet path Eco-Nick took. Which way do you go?

❀ ❀ ❀ ❀ ❀ ❀ ❀

Search the Sticky Bubble Chews factory on page 199
Hunt for Jumping Chocolate Caterpillars on page 203
Find the Sour Power factory on page 204

The Giz uses his Super Sniffer to find the Garden of Eve Farm. You, the kids, and Coco follow him.

A little boy in a pumpkin waves to you from the front gate. "My name is Forest and my parents own this farm."

Forest is a great name for a farmer's son! You write it on your reporter's e-pad.

"We're looking for Eco-Nick, the tasty wizard," Daisy says. "Do you know where he is?"

Forest giggles. "Eco-Nick comes here all the time."

"Why?" you ask.

"The Garden of Eve is organic," Forest says. "That means we don't use any nasty bug sprays, weed killers, or chemicals."

"What's the big deal?" Bob grumbles.

"The earth likes us," Forest explains. "We don't pollute the air, water, or soil. We grow fruits, vegetables, crops, and flowers that are good for the earth, animals, and people!"

"Don't all farms do that?" you ask.

"No," Forest replies sadly. "If all the Toxic Town farms were organic, everything would be cleaner."

"Maybe I can use my Amazing Tail Zap to make all the

Toxic Town farms go organic," Coco yelps.

"No!" you and The Giz cry.

"We can get our parents to buy organic farm food that will help clean up Toxic Town!" Daisy hollers.

"That's a much better idea," you and The Giz agree.

Coco looks insulted.

160

Suddenly, a lot of animals appear right in front of you. There are cows, sheep, goats, chickens, and turkeys. There are even two cute little dogs herding the animals. Eco-Nick jumps out of the middle of the animals. He has a new wand that looks like a celery stick.

"We found you!" Everyone cries.

Eco-Nick laughs. "That Twisted Spaghetti Wizard stuff was all a pile of poop," he says. "The kids had to take action."

You get it. The Twisted Spaghetti Wizard was Eco-Nick's act. He used it so the kids from Toxic Town would take action. Now the kids know that eating green food makes the earth happy. They'll visit Forest and the Garden of Eve Farm all the time! Toxic Town will be cleaner, and it won't have to shut down. The town may even get clean enough to change its name!

Everyone cheers as Eco-Nick dips his celery stick wand into a bowl of Forest's favorite cheese dip.

🐾 🐾 🐾 🐾 🐾 🐾 🐾

Visit Forest's real family at the Garden of Eve on page 210
Meet the real Eco-Nick on page 208

South Carolina waste-to-energy plant that converts landfill gas to electricity

Compliments of The United States Environmental Protection Agency

162

Be a water buddy!

Humans are responsible for everything that ends up in our water. It's up to you to keep our water clean.

Water from rain and melting snow flows into the streets. Along the way, this water picks up candy wrappers, cigarette butts, trash, chemicals, and even pet poop. It travels along the gutters into sewers, lakes, rivers, and streams. These are the same waters we use for drinking, bathing, swimming, and fishing.

<u>Don't</u> pour chemicals down sinks, toilets, or drains.
Household chemicals like paint, cleaning spray, weed killer, bug killer, and perfume, should never end up in our water.

<u>Don't</u> flush sandwich baggies or band-aids down the toilet.
They're not biodegradable, and don't break down naturally. They wind up littering beaches and rivers.

<u>Do</u> replace toxic chemicals at home with nontoxic products.
Use safe products that don't put unhealthy chemicals in our water. Not throwing them down the drain helps, but not buying them in the first place is better.

<u>Do</u> use fertilizers like compost, manure, bone meal or peat.
Composting, and natural fertilizers decrease the need for fertilizer and help soil keep its moisture.

Fuel that makes the earth happy!

Coco and The Giz thank our green sponsors for
helping us spread the word

Annie's Homegrown
Ecoist
Garden of Eve Farm
Healthy Home Products
News12 Long Island
Espresso Book Machine
Thomson-Shore
Tri-State Biodiesel

Coco and The Giz thank our educational grant foundations for making our book possible

**Best Buy Te@ch
BOCES Arts-in-Education
East End Arts Council
Lowe's Toolbox for Education
Owl Teacher Center
Newsday FutureCorps
Target Foundation**

New York State Assembly
Albany, New York

To: Isiah and his fellow students
Parliament Place Elementary School
North Babylon, New York

Thanks for telling me about the Go Green! program at the Parliament Place Elementary School.

Soon after I received your card, I became the new chairman of the New York State Assembly's Environmental Conservation Committee. I hope to do many things to help protect our environment.

One of the first things I did was to get $200,000 in the new state budget for Belmont Lake State Park in North Babylon, to help control aquatic growth and invasive species in the lake. Those are plants in the water that are not native to this area, and can crowd out plants that are natural to Belmont. This new money will help bring that population under control.

Thanks to you and your classmates for all you are doing to go green, and please keep me posted on your efforts.

Very truly yours,

Robert K. Sweeney
New York State Assembly

Solar panels on the roof

Coco and The Giz help KEYSPAN Kids save energy now!

Turn off the lights so the dust mites don't fight.

Get really bright with fluorescent light

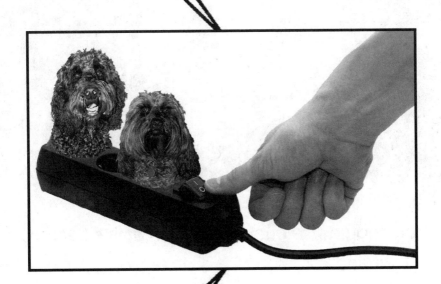

Plant a tree for mini me!

Power down when you're out of town.

Ms. Fossil Face's letters are from kids around the world!

Dear Ms. Fossil Face,

You should use energy from windmills because it's clean and you won't be a dirty blob. It's more fun being a clean blob. Clean blobs rule the world!

Dear Ms. Fossil Face,

You should get some windmills and make a windmill farm. You can also put some solar power panels around, like the ones on The Willow Pet Hotel and store the electricity until we need it.

Dear Ms. Fossil Face,

If you use clean energy like windmills, solar panels, and water power, you won't get dirty. You can help the earth live, if you do the right thing!

Dear Ms. Fossil Face,

You can put pretty flower windmills outside in a windy place and solar power panels on the roof under the hot sun. Our school can have electricity and you can be one pretty blob again.

Write an e-mail to Ms. Fossil Face at
www.greenletters@bookwebpublishing.com.
She'll post it online for people and blobs to see.

Meet the Keyspan Kids on page 169

"We can build a windmill," you shout. "The Dirty Energy Creeps will run away when they see how clean it is. You'll get your job back!"

"You'll be pretty again," The Giz says.

Coco yelps and spits some red-hot sparkles on Ms. Fossil Face. It looks good on the unhappy blob.

You know that wind is a great way to make energy. Wind power has been used to sail boats and grind wheat and corn. Wind can also make electricity. It's really simple - just like blowing on a pinwheel. The wind turns the blades in the windmill. The blades turn a machine that makes electricity. Most important - Dirty Energy Creeps hate windmills!

You grab your reporter's e-pad. This story will write itself!

"I can do it!" Coco barks happily. She drops the pink pointy hat with red-hot sparkles. There's a small pile of used napkins. Coco fires her Amazing Tail Zap at the napkins!

The napkins turn into . . . a rubber ducky.

You, Ms. Fossil Face, and The Giz laugh.

"I'm not perfect!" Coco yaps. She fires her Amazing Tail Zap at the rubber ducky.

The rubber ducky turns into . . . blue gummy worms.

You, The Giz, and Ms. Fossil Face eat the blue gummy worms. They're really yummy.

"I have to work on that Amazing Tail Zap stuff," Coco whimpers, picking up the pink, pointy hat with red-hot sparkles.

"Why don't you build the windmills," The Giz says to

Ms. Fossil Face. "If you build enough of them, you'll have clean electricity for everyone!"

"You'll be the most beautiful blob in the world again," you cheer, writing notes on your reporter's e-pad.

At last, Coco drops the pink, pointy hat with red-hot sparkles. Her Amazing Tail Zap gave her enough blue gummy worms to bring along to the windmill farm.

Welcome to Hoover Dam!

Hoover Dam is a hydroelectric project. It makes enough electricity to supply a city of 750,000 people!

A large dam "plugs" a river. It forces the water to form a deep pool. Hoover Dam plugs the Colorado River, creating a "pool" called Lake Mead - in the desert! Lake Mead is a fun place to go swimming, boating, and fishing. It's the largest man-made lake in the United States.

The plugged up water has a lot of pressure. It's like a water balloon - if you pop it, everything comes rushing out.

174

Hoover Dam uses the water pressure to turn big turbines or machines that make electricity. Turbines look like this.

Facts about Hoover Dam

*Hoover Dam opened in 1936. It's located in two states - Arizona and Nevada.

*During its busiest time, enough water runs through the dam to fill 15 swimming pools in ONE SECOND.

*The base of Hoover Dam is as thick as two football fields lying end-to-end.

*At 726 feet tall, Hoover Dam is the second highest dam in the United States - and taller than the Washington Monument!

*It cost $165,000,000 to build Hoover Dam.

It's the wildest racetrack you've ever seen!
There are hundreds of cars everywhere.
Their engines are idling, waiting to
begin the race. The GasGuys make a
lot of noise and smoke. They
leave a trail of yucky, leaking oil.
The HyBrids are very quiet.
Everyone loves them.

The GreenWheels make the sun shine
brighter.

"Would you like to ride with me?" Ethie whispers to you.

It's the chance of a lifetime! You jump into the front seat,
put on your helmet, and snap on the seatbelt. Ethie is amazing.
Her seats are racing orange and black leather. The dashboard is
filled with bright buttons, dials, and gadgets.

"Don't touch," Ethie warns, "except for stuff like the pizza
button."

"Sure." You say, taking out your reporter's e-pad.

"It's a long race," Ethie reminds you. "Two days, thirty
minutes, and twenty seconds. Don't worry, it goes quickly."

Now you know why there are buttons for foods like a
Happy Meal, Egg McMuffin, and a
Quarter Pounder!

Before you can say anything, the
green flag is up! There's an
earsplitting roar. You and Ethie
begin the most amazing car race
ever.

Race to the finish on the next page ➡️

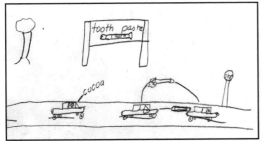

It's the fastest race of your life!

In the beginning, it's a road race. You fly past Sticky's Sugar Shack and Fuzzy's Toothpaste. Gooey's Gloppy Grasslands are filled with human kids and Brenna's Place is growing organic cookies for dogs. You wish you could make a quick stop at Jamie's Candy Corn Farm or Michael's Popcorn Place.

Suddenly, all of the cars are bumper-to-bumper in a very dark tunnel. At the end of the tunnel is Gizco Volcano - with a fire-breathing dragon and a giant, one-eyed Cyclops. Ethie dodges them without a problem. A lot of the cars get stuck there and drop out of the race!

The road ends and the race continues in the ocean. Ethie pops out her sails. She's in the lead - until you see a brick wall in the middle of the water. There's a big sign on the wall.

Time to Fly

Some cars can't make it past the sign. Ethie has no problem. She flies like a bird.

The race is really long. You watch the sun set and the sun rise two times. Ethie makes her pit stops. You eat a Big Mac and a lot of apple dippers.

Finally, there are twenty seconds to go! Three cars are left in the race - Ethie, Zappy, Ben, and Shredder.

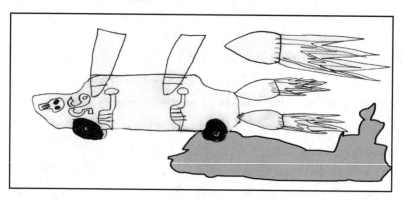

Ethie is in the lead!

Without warning, Shredder dumps strawberry slime on the road. The cars slip and slide as Shredder pulls into the lead. Ethie rises into the air and hovers over the slime. Everyone else falls behind.

The race is now between Ethie and Shredder.

Shredder spits out a cloud of blue cotton candy and Ethie can't see a thing. Shredder is going to win!

Out of nowhere, Dr. GreenWheels, Coco, and The Giz appear above the blue cotton candy.

"Go for it," The Giz barks from the sunroof.

Coco blows her Sanitizing Breath. The blue cotton candy is still there . . . but now it's so clean, you can see right through it. Not bad for a superhero-in-training.

Ethie zooms through the blue cotton candy into first place!

Gizco Island is out of control! The cheers are so loud that the whales in the ocean can hear them. Everyone honks Ethie's name.

Ethie glides into the winner's circle to get her prize.

You hug Coco. "You did it, Coco-nutty," you shout.

Coco opens her mouth to lick you and a puff of blue cotton candy flies in your face.

"Ooops," Coco yaps.

The end of the most amazing car race ever.

Oiler is ready to go! He lines up to start the race. He revs his engines and the delicious odor of food takes over.

Oiler smells like a fillet-o-fish with large fries! The kids can't get enough of him. They hang all over Oiler. He can't move an inch.

The green flag goes up and Oiler never gets past the starting line, but he makes a lot of kids and dogs very happy.

The end of this yummy adventure.

The Orbiter Space Shuttle

Everyone is safe! No one wants to be a dragonfly's dinner.

Now you understand why gas is a problem. If you use up all the oil in the earth, where will gas come from? Fossil fuels like oil are non-renewable. Once you use them up, you can't make anymore.

You grab your reporter's e-pad. There's more to the story. Using gas as fuel is bad for the earth. It causes global warming which makes the earth hotter and changes the weather. A lot of bad things can happen. The ice melts and animals, like polar bears and penguins, have no place to live. Sometimes, there's no rain and people run out of water. Storms like hurricanes and tornados are worse and do a lot of damage. The list is endless!

Shredder is very sad. "I don't want to make the earth sick," he says, "but I need gas to run the race."

Which way do you go?

❧ ❧ ❧ ❧ ❧ ❧ ❧

Pump gas on page 211
Mix up the stuff on page 213

Coco and The Giz thank our special program supporters.

Parliament Place School PTA
Suffolk Reading Council
PARP
North Babylon District Business Office
Babylon Town Supervisor Steve Bellone
Babylon Town Energy Director Dorian Gray
Officer George Lynagh,
Suffolk County Police Department

You jump in the plastic, but suddenly it's not there. You try to save the little boy, but he's gone too.

"What's wrong?" you ask E-Wiz. "Why can't I touch him?"

E-Wiz shrugs. "I'm a wizard not a travel agent. I can't take everyone along on my wizard trips. I can only make it *feel* real. It's a huge E-Wiz screen with smell!"

It still tricks your human mind to think that you're smack in the middle of a wizard trip on the other side of the world. The little boy is in trouble, but you can't do anything.

Coco takes a flying leap at you. She lands on your shoulders and does a full face wash with her tongue, getting rid of the dirt that's not really there.

It's better than an Amazing Tail Zap.

The end of this wizard travel adventure.

"Do something!" you cry.

E-Wiz touches your shoulder with his wand that now looks like a crunchy computer chip.

Everyone is right back in Toxic Town School.

"It starts here," E-Wiz points to the printer next to the computer.

"I don't understand," Daisy wails.

E-Wiz opens the cover on the printer. "This is a printer ink cartridge," he says. "It's where the ink is stored. That's how you can print stuff from the computer."

Everyone looks at the black plastic printer cartridge.

"What does that have to do with the little boy on the other side of the world?" you ask.

"Every second, less time than it takes to say this sentence, 8 printer cartridges are thrown out. That's about 350 million cartridges a year."

"Yes!" Daisy says. "I've seen piles of them in the Toxic Town landfill."

E-Wiz nods wisely. "When cartridges go to a landfill . . . or to the other side of the world, they stay there for 450 years! The plastic doesn't rot or decompose. Some parts last for a thousand years."

Everyone is very quiet.

185

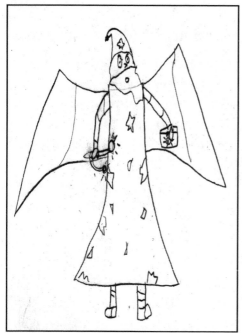

"If all the cartridges thrown out in one year were lined up end-to-end, they would go around earth three times," E-Wiz adds.

"Why can't people recycle them?" you ask.

"They can," E-Wiz says sadly. "They just have to go to the right place."

"I don't understand," you frown.

"People who don't care about the earth just dump old printer cartridges. A lot of kids get sick from the pollution - like the little boy on the other side of the world. Mean people don't care."

"Is there anything we can do to help Toxic Town and the other side of the world?"

E-Wiz nods. "Meet Mr. World."

Which way do you go?

Meet Mr. Cartridge World on page 219
Run away from all that nasty plastic on page 222
See the real kid on the other side of the world on page 218

T-Shore the tree kid looks like a walking tree. She has branches instead of arms and leaves instead of hands. Coco sniffs her trunk and gets a whack from her lowest branch. Leaping in the air, Coco prepares to fire her Amazing Tail Zap. The Giz catches her before it's too late, and pins her to the ground.

"Not now," The Giz snarls.

E-Wiz watches everything from one of T-shore's highest branches. He looks like a monkey from a picture book.

"Books begin with authors," T-shore says. Her words sound like blowing leaves on a windy day. She gives Coco a dirty look. "Would you like to meet some?"

The kids cheer.

"These are some of the authors who wrote a book called *Coco and The Giz Go Green*," T-shore says proudly. "It's about making the earth healthy."

Meet some student-authors on the next page

The Which Way
Student-Authors at work

189

Coco and The Giz bark. You take out your reporter's e-pad and start writing.

"The authors asked me to print their book," T-shore continues, "because I'm a tree kid."

T-shore shakes her leaves.

"Trees are very important to the earth," T-shore says. "They keep the air, water, and soil clean. They also give people and dogs food like fruit and nuts. People use wood from trees to make things like houses, furniture, and toys."

Coco yelps.

"Okay," T-shore says, "dogs like to chew on branches because it keeps their teeth clean."

That sounds like more fun than a toothbrush, you think.

"Things you use everyday come from trees," T-shore continues, "that you never know about!"

"Yowwwww," E-Wiz dangles from a branch overhead. "Cereals, paint, nail polish, pancake syrup . . . even your toilet seat comes from trees! Trees make my bubblegum chewier," E-Wiz giggles as he blows a trail of pink bubbles.

You write everything down on your reporter's e-pad.

"Over the years, the earth has lost most of her forests because people cut down trees for things like paper, furniture, and buildings," adds T-shore. "They

190

also cut down forests to grow crops and raise animals. When the forests no longer have trees, the climate changes and global warming gets worse."

"The earth gets hotter," The Giz woofs.

Global warming is very bad for the earth., you write on your e-pad.

"When we make books," T-shore grins,  "we use recycled paper that would have gone to the landfill. We save trees!"

The kids cheer.

"That's not all," T-shore adds. 'We recycle all our own paper, as well as printing plates, printing waste, and oil. The T-shores are the earth-happiest bookmakers in the country!"

The kids roar even louder.

Which way do you want to go?

🐾 🐾 🐾 🐾 🐾 🐾 🐾

Visit T-shore's home on page 223
See how a T-shore book makes the earth happy on page 224
Read a real T-shore book on page 11

Espresso looks more like a machine than a critic.

"What's that?" you ask E-Wiz.

E-Wiz transforms into a giant green music player with an earphone wand.

You, the kids, Coco, and The Giz crowd around Espresso.

"You can talk to me," Espresso says grumpily.

"Sorry," you apologize. "I didn't think you're . . . someone."

"Ehhhhhh," Espresso mumbles, "most people don't know about me at all, but they will!"

"What are you?" Coco yelps, leaping onto Espresso's plastic skin.

"Don't touch me," Espresso snaps, "your paws are dirty."
Coco backs away.

"I'm magic," Espresso continues. "I make a book in less time than it takes to make a fluffer nutter.

Everyone knows that a fluffer nutter is a sandwich made from marshmallow cream and peanut butter. Mmmmm . . . you can use one now.

Espresso makes strange whirring sounds. You hear clinks and clunks.

You have no clue what Espresso is doing, but it doesn't sound or smell very fluffer nutter-ish.

"Watch," E-Wiz grins, reading your thoughts.

Suddenly Espresso sighs loudly and spits out a . . . book!

You pick up the book, and it's a copy of *Coco and The Giz Go Green*.

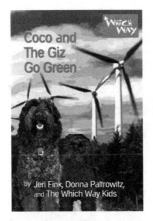

"I make books when you want them," Espresso laughs. "You push some buttons, and there's your book."

It's hard to believe. You look at the book in your hand. *Coco and The Giz Go Green* is the real thing.

E-Wiz laughs like a crazed rocker.

"I do it all," Espresso boasts. "I'm the best!"

"That's really cool," you say. "How does it make the earth happy?"

"Write this down on your reporter's e-pad," Espresso says. "I make one book at a time. Books don't have to be shipped by trucks and airplanes that pollute the air. People get books only when they need them - we don't have to throw out extra books in the landfill. The paper we use is recycled, so we're saving trees at the same time!"

You look at Espresso with new respect. He's awesome!

🐾 🐾 🐾 🐾 🐾 🐾 🐾

See the real Espresso in action on page 225

Compact Fluorescent Light Bulbs

It's a REAL magic bulb. If every American home used just ONE compact fluorescent light bulb, we would save enough energy to light more than 2.5 million homes for a year.

Babylon Town Supervisor Steve Bellone (above) and Babylon Town Energy Director Dorian Gray (below) explain the power of compact fluorescent light bulbs to the North Babylon kids.

194

Mr. Luna's Bright Idea

Mr. Luna and our student-authors from
Robert Moses Middle School are working to give every child in
America just ONE compact fluorescent bulb to plug in at home.
It would put all America on the right environmental path.

Meet the rest of the kids on the next page ➡

Coco and The Giz thank the Robert Moses Middle School Which Way student-authors

Adam Amin
Akil Barrett
Alejandra Rua-Llano
Alexis Schmohl
Alyssa Allgaier
Amanda Conner
Amrita Dubay
Anthony Caruso
Anthony Mirrione
Anthony Mulder
Anthony Ricciardi
Argenis Vasquez
Ashley Mascaro
Brendan Walshe
Brett Rufrano
Brianna Addison
Cassandra Clairmont
Charles Kuhn
Chelsea Demetriou
Christine Dadabo
Christopher Cruz
Craig Williams
Daniel Clancy
David Ferer
Elena Bavaro
Fredrick Hilker
Gina Marie Mancuso
Golden Ukonu
James Leonard
Jamie Calo
Jared Goldstein
Jean Paul Massip
Jelani Mack

John Ciura
John Hughes
John McGrath
Joseph Martin
Joseph Scaduto
Joseph Sciangula
Kaitlyn Beck
Kamali O'Brian
Karina Perez
Kayla Marzo
Keith Drescher
Kevin Chase Henry
Kimberly Hayes
Kristen Ford
Leonard Matias
Louis Feis
Manuel Cosenza
Maria Ivanoff
Marianne Licciardi
Melissa Armenia
Melissa Berrick
Michael Baquiran
Michael Reha
Michelle Gioielli
Nabiha Rahaman
Na'eemah Lewter
Mathalia Andrade
Nigel Campbell
Nicholas Barsalona
Nicholas Bucicchia
Nicholas Rudy
Nicole Earl
Nicole Kaplan

Nicole Kear
Nicole Lupia
Nicole Marzocca
Nicole Wenke
Oldy Jean
Owen Kelly
Peter Brady
Rayshawn Perry
Raymond Zizzo
Riley John Munro
Robert Chevallier
Russell Frisby
Ryan Fackner
Ryan Levine
Sean Simoes
Shaheen Carr
Shaina Parker
Shavonne Rogers
Steven Palumbo
Sulliman Noor
Shinelle Tyson
Tanesha Muracin
Taylor Cress
Taylor Scaraglino
Teresa Lewandoswki
Thomas Bennett
Thomas Levy
Tianna Moorer
Tricia Davila
Vincent Cuomo
Vincent Scanapico
Whitney Mimms
William Washington

196

Meet the real CeeKay

Mrs. Kuchta, Principal
Parliament Place School
North Babylon, New York

Save our friends from
global warming!

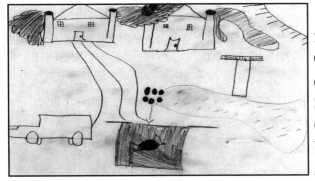

You, the kids from Toxic Town, Coco, and The Giz charge into the Sticky Bubble Chews Factory. The big machines buzz and the smell of candy is everywhere. Everyone loves Sticky Bubble Chews - people candy for dogs. People and dogs both eat these tasty treats. You see the recipe for Sticky Bubble Chews on the wall in the factory:

The Secret Recipe and directions for Sticky Bubble Chews

1. soak hot dogs in lots of sugar
2. mix in bananas (no peels)
3. add sticky string bean mush
4. throw in a bucket of turkey gravy
5. mix well and shape into bones
6. bake until it makes really big sticky, chewy bubbles

"Where's Eco-Nick?" you cry.

"Leave it to me," The Giz says. He uses his Super Sniffer to search for the wizard.

"Eco-Nick isn't here," The Giz says when he finishes.

You don't need Eco-Nick to tell you why the factory is so nasty! There are piles of yucky, leftover, hot dog pieces in the corners. Rotten banana peels are knee-deep against the wall. Sticky, string bean mush is in leaky, overflowing pails. The turkey gravy looks like a poop carpet.

"I'm getting my paws dirty in this muck," Coco yelps.

"Stuff it," a tall, round man suddenly appears. He has a big head, a tiny nose, and an apron covered with Sticky Bubble Chews stains.

"Who are you?" The Giz asks.

"I'm the owner," Apron-man says. "Get out of here."

"You don't talk to The Giz like that," Coco yaps. She leaps at Apron-man, but misses by a paw.

"This place must go green," you say to Apron-man.

"I own this place," Apron-man says. "I can do what I want." He pats Coco on the head. "I like you, dog. You have spunk."

Coco barks fiercely. She sounds more like a fluffy, pink toy poodle than a superhero-in-training.

"Anyway," Apron-man adds, "Sticky Bubble Chews aren't green."

"Compost," you holler.

"What's compost?" Apron-man asks.

"Compost is a pile of stuff that helps farmers, gardeners, and the earth," you explain.

He ignores you. "Are you a fifth grader in a fur coat or a fuzzy superhero?" Apron-man asks The Giz.

The Giz is not happy. "I'm Earth's Superhero," he roars. "Show some respect."

"Sorry," Apron-man mumbles.

"This factory wastes too much stuff," The Giz snarls. "Think of it this way. More than 96 billion pounds of food goes to waste every year."

"You mean," the owner looks around, "like all the hot dog pieces, banana peels, leftover string bean mush, and turkey gravy?"

"Yes! Add coffee grounds, leftover lunches, stale donuts, and the melted chocolate fingers you hide in your office. That's a lot of wasted food," you say.

"It all goes into the landfill and makes Toxic Town worse," The Giz barks.

"Here's what you can do," you suggest. "Take all that stuff and dump it in a big bin. Mix in some earthworms, and it turns into compost all by itself. You can use the compost to grow gardens all over town."

"Your factory would be clean, the landfill would be smaller, and the compost will grow daisies on Factory Street," The Giz adds.

"You can also send compost to farms, gardeners, even to the Toxic Town School soccer field to make the grass grow better!" You grin.

"Wow!" Apron-man bellows. "I'm going to get started right now. If all these kids help me, I'll give out free Sticky Bubble Chews."

Apron-man points to large wooden bins outside the factory. He writes the word COMPOST on each bin. Everyone is really excited. Apron-man has set up the first compost bins on Factory Street.

Eco-Nick has done his magic wihout even showing up!

The end of this adventure and the beginning of "green" Sticky Bubble Chews.

You, the kids, Coco, and The Giz wade through piles of mucky trash. You missed the Jumping Chocolate Caterpillars because they left Toxic Town in a hurry. They couldn't stand the pollution. The door to the factory is locked. There's a sign on the door, but you have to get very close to some creepy crawlies to read it.

Too smelly to stay. Even Eco-Nick couldn't stand it. Go home while you can.

The end of this creepy adventure.

The sign is right in front of you.
Welcome to Sour Power!
It's the factory that makes your favorite Sour Power candy.

Is Eco-Nick inside the Sour Power Factory?

You decide to have a Sour Power before going inside. First, you take the box from your pocket. You open the box and there's a crinkly plastic bag. You tear the plastic bag and reach inside for a Sour Power.

The candy has a pretty outer wrapper. You twist it off and . . . there's an inner wrapper. By the time you finish, there's more packaging than candy.

Everyone stares at the pile of garbage in your hand.
"All that packaging goes to the landfill," you say softly.
"Wouldn't it be great if we could get Sour Powers without

all the garbage?" Bob says.

"It would make a lot of kids happy . . . and keep a lot of garbage out of the landfill!" Daisy adds.

"I know," you shout. "What if Sour Power used wrappers that we can eat . . . like rice paper?"

Everyone cheered.

"The other Sour Power wrappers could be recycled" you add.

Suddenly there's lightning and thunder. Your heart pounds in fear. The Twisted Spaghetti Wizard appears out of thin air. He's the one who stole Eco-Nick.

"Get him!" you shout.

"Hold your pancakes," someone says.

You turn around, and there's Eco-Nick with a brand new red licorice wand.

Everyone screams.

"Cool it," Eco-Nick says. "I wasn't really missing. The Twisted Spaghetti Wizard is really my buddy. We do this disappearing act to help kids take action."

You groan.

"Wizards are great," Eco-Nick explains, "but kids are better. When you take action it really sticks. Twisted Spaghetti Wizard and I like to help stir things up, if you know what I mean."

"No." Daisy cries. "We haven't done anything."

"Not yet," Eco-Nick takes a big bite out of his red licorice wand. "You have the idea."

Eco-Nick points to your hand. It's still filled with the packaging from your Sour Power. "Cut the packaging,"

Eco-Nick grins, "and you'll clean up Toxic Town."

"Okay," you grumble. You don't like being tricked, even if he is a wizard. "What should we do with it?"

"Meet my friend, Ecoist," Eco-Nick says proudly.

❀ ❀ ❀ ❀ ❀ ❀ ❀

Munch on chocolate jelly feet on page 226
Hang out with Ecoist on page 227

Coco and The Giz thank all our amazing educators at Parliament Place School.

Kindergarten
KA A. Jackson
KB K. Raucci
KC L. Rodriguez
KD M. Cox

First Grade
1A L. Urban
1B S. Widecki
1C K. Henn
1D D. Dooley

Second Grade
2A J. Thomas
2B A. Montuori
2C M. Ivy
2D S. Bachety

Third Grade
3A J. Gross
3B L. Hoogervorst
3C D. Heins
3E S. Molinelli

Fourth Grade
4A M. Brennan
4B L. Bonacci
4C S. Manning

Fifth Grade
5A W. Keese
5B G. Morisie
5C D. McCabe
5D T. Jacquemain
5E P. O'Brien

Registered Nurse
M. Melicharek

Art
R. Blank

Media Specialist
K. Quigley

Physical Education
M. Kelly
A. Lewis

Instrumental Music
A. McInerney/Band
N. Verderosa/Orchestra

Resource Room
S. Heaney
J. Gryn

Perm. Substitute
L. LaRocco

Vocal Music
L. Hopkins

Math
K. Dein

Psychologist
M. Reynolds

Reading
M. Davis
G. Coyle

Social Worker
R. Adler

Speech
R. Schild

The Real Eco-Nick
Nick LaRocco

Polar bears need ice.
Stop climate change now!

Meet Forest's real family at the Garden of Eve

Compliments of Garden of Eve Farm
www.gardenofevefarm.com

Shredder takes You, Coco, and The Giz to a nearby gas station with rows of gas pumps.

"Usually this place has cars lined up for gas," Shredder explains.

"Everyone is all gassed up," Coco yaks. She leaps into the air and tries to catch her tail. She misses it by a paw.

"Where is everyone?" You ask.

"Read the sign," Shredder grumbles.

No gas! We ran out of 100-foot high plants, 2-foot long dragonflies, and 6-foot long caterpillars with a zillion legs a few hundred million years ago.

You've run out of gas and time.

🐾 🐾 🐾 🐾 🐾 🐾 🐾

Get some chocolate jelly feet on page 226

The Real Prius

Compliments of Atlantic Toyota
www.atlantictoyotascion.com

Shredder is really sad. There has to be a way to get enough gas so he can be in the Bone Challenge. You think really hard.

"I've got it," you shout. "I know how to get enough gas for the race."

"How?" Shredder shifts gears.

"Use mixed gas," you reply.

"I can't use mixed gas," Shredder replies. "I'm a GasGuy."

"Yes, you can!" You, Coco, and The Giz jump inside Shredder. You make sure not to push the green time machine button. "Take us to the New Gas Station!"

Shredder takes you to the station. You jump out and search the gas pumps.

"Here it is!" You say proudly. You point to a gas pump that has a tiny sign on the front: 10% Ethanol

"What does that mean?" Shredder asks.

"This fuel mixes gas and ethanol. Ethanol is a renewable fuel that's made from stuff like corn and sugar cane. You can grow it every year so it never runs out."

"Will it work?" Shredder sounds unsure.

"You won't know the difference," you grin. "At the same time it makes the earth happier because you're using less fossil fuel. Any GasGuy can use it."

"Let's do it!" Shredder pops open his gas tank.

Race with Shredder on the next page ➡

It's race time!

Shredder revs his engine and moves toward the starting line. He's ready to win, fueled with gas and ethanol.

Out of the blue, he stops.

"I want you to race with me," Shredder says.

Your eyes pop. Race with Shredder in the Bone Challenge? It's the most exciting thing in world!

You leap inside Shredder. Coco and The Giz give you a bag full of Happy Meals and apple dippers. You pull out your reporter's e-pad.

"It's a long race," Coco says. "You'll get hungry."

Two days, thirty minutes, and twenty seconds on the road is a very long time. You quickly learn that you won't be spending the whole time on the road.

The cars begin by doing two laps around the racetrack. This will be easy, you think. Shredder is in the group of six lead cars.

The road heads out of the racetrack. You pass Fred's Orchard, Apple City, and Michael's Sunny Farm. You grab some fat plump apples from Zedia's Farm Stand and drool over Ivy's apple pies. You wonder what's cooking at Ryan's Going Green Kitchen.

Everything starts to change. Shredder races through a narrow cave where it's really easy to crash into the rocks. On the other side is a jungle filled with scary animals. You don't worry. No one can catch Shredder.

By the time you see the ocean, there are a lot less cars in the race. You don't want to think about what happened to them. Shredder plunges deep into the water. You see a large school of yellow-and-orange fish. They need help! They can't find their way home.

Shredder slows down. He leads the fish home. The fish are safe, but now Shredder is in last place. How can he win? Wait. The yellow-and-orange fish are pointing to something.

There's a large underwater rock with writing. You read the

word painted on the rock.

FLY!

Shredder knows just what to do. He races through the water like a missile. Before you know it, there's a big splash and Shredder is flying!

Your heart pounds like crazy. This is the most amazing race ever!

Two days and thirty minutes go by in a flash. The sun rises and sets twice. You know the race is almost over because all your food is gone.

There are only three cars left. Shredder is last.

If Shredder didn't save the fish, he would be in the lead. Now there are only twenty seconds to go. You know he can't win.

Suddenly, Shredder takes a very deep car breath. He leaps forward. He reaches the rear bumper of the car in second place. Then he passes it! Shredder is now in second. There's only one lap left.

The black-checkered flag is waiting for the winner. Shredder gets closer to the lead car.

"You can do it," you scream.

With one last burst of energy, Shredder pulls ahead.

Shredder wins the Annual Bone Challenge by a bumper!

Cars, dogs, and people cheer. The noise is so loud it hurts your ears. Everyone is so happy! Even the earth feels a little bit better because Shredder won with mixed gas!

The crowd throws green popcorn to celebrate. Shredder zips through it, honking wildly.

Everyone screams Shredder's name.

Shredder races into the winner's circle to get his prize.

You jump out and hug Coco and The Giz. "We won!" you shout.

Coco fires her Amazing Tail Zap. Suddenly you're covered in bubblegum spit.

"Want a free face wash?" Coco offers, ready to lick.

The surprise ending to this mixed-up adventure.

The real boy from Guiya, China. He sits on top of a pile of toxic printer cartridges and computer waste brought in from around the world.

Compliments of Basel Action Network, 2006.

Mr. Cartridge World is just a regular guy who cares about the earth. He can be found in many towns across the country and around the world. People call him Mr. World. He's not even a wizard.

"Mr. World reuses, refills, and recycles printer cartridges right here," E-Wiz explains. "When you bring your printer ink cartridges to him, they never end up in the Toxic Town landfill or on the other side of the world."

"You save the earth, the kids, and money," Mr. World adds, "just by doing the right thing."

"Let's do it," you cry. "We'll get everyone in Toxic Town to bring their printer ink cartridges to Mr. World!"

All the kids cheer.

The little boy on the other side of the world cheers too.

See the real Cartridge World on the next page ➡️

The student-authors at Parliament Place School collected ink cartridges from their school, families, and community. They worked with Cartridge World, U.S.A. to make sure that the cartridges were recycled.

Can you find Earth's Superheroes in this photo?

Cartridge World, U.S.A.
www.cartridgeworldusa.com

You don't want to think about the boy on the other side of the world. You run away.

This printer is . . . running . . . out . . . of . . . ink . . .

Blank pages are no fun! This is really the end for you!

❀ ❀ ❀ ❀ ❀ ❀ ❀

Meet Mr. Cartridge World on page 219

The real Thomson-Shore

www.tshore.com

green
press
INITIATIVE

Book Web Publishing, Ltd. is committed to preserving ancient forests and natural resources. We elected to print *Which Way?* on 30% post consumer recycled paper, processed chlorine free. As a result, for this printing, we have saved:

10 Trees (40' tall and 6-8" diameter)
4,357 Gallons of Waste Water
1,752 Kilowatt Hours of Electricity
480 Pounds of Solid Waste
943 Pounds of Greenhouse Gases

Book Web Publishing, Ltd. made this paper choice because our printer, Thomson-Shore, Inc., is a member of Green Press Initiative, a nonprofit program dedicated to supporting authors, publishers, and suppliers in their efforts to reduce their use of fiber obtained from endangered forests.

For more information, visit www.greenpressinitiative.org

The real Espresso Book Machine
The machine produces 15-20 quality paperbacks per hour, in any language, in quantities of one!
www.ondemandbooks.com

When you're sad or angry, there's nothing better than chocolate. You dig up a whole box of chocolate jelly feet. They taste great. Too bad those mushy feet get stuck to your teeth. Ouch! It's time to visit the dentist.

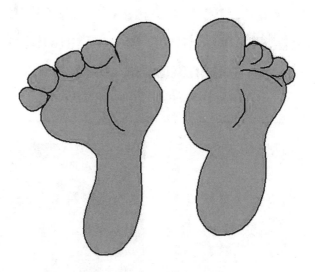

The end of this toothy adventure.

Ecoist looks like a regular kid, except for all her pocketbooks, purses, and tote bags. The bags hang from her neck, shoulders, and elbows.

She smiles at you, the kids from Toxic Town, Coco, and The Giz.

Eco-Nick chews on his red licorice wand while he watches. Twisted Spaghetti Wizard slurp on a Sour Power.

"Here's what we can do with all those candy wrappers," Ecoist says.

She holds up a brightly-colored bag. "This was made from old Sour Power candy wrappers!"

"This was made from candy wrappers, too!"

Coco somersaults over the bags.

"They're so pretty," Daisy says. "Can I have one?"

Before you know it, all the kids from Toxic Town want their own Ecoist bags.

"Lots of trees are used to make the paper wrappers for candy that get thrown away in the landfills," Ecoist explains. "Sometimes there are extra wrappers that are never used and get tossed away. Instead of wasting the paper, these wrappers make special bags."

"The planet stays cleaner, and I get a cool bag," Daisy giggles.

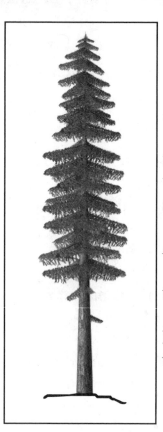

"To keep the planet healthy, every time we make a new candy wrapper bag, we plant a tree for the earth," Ecoist smiles.

Now there's a great story for *Book Web News!*

"Can I have a candy wrapper bag too?" Coco yelps.

"I have something else for you," Ecoist laughs. "It's made from the pop tops on soda cans."

Turn to the next page ▶

229

Find the names

Visit Coco and The Giz online!
www.bookwebpublishing.com

There's so much to do when you visit our website!

*Meet more student authors
*Check out other books by kids
*See how kids write books
*Get free Coco and The Giz stuff
*Write Coco and The Giz e-mails
*Send free Coco and The Giz e-cards
*See Coco and The Giz puppy pictures
*Make The Giz bark
*and much more!

Coco and The Giz
Go Game!

Turn to the next page ➤

Who are these critters?

Clues

* The guy with the sunglasses weighs 50 pounds more than the girl with the pointy hat.

*The girl with the pointy hat rules.

*The guy with the sunglasses loves peanut butter; the girl with the pointy hat loves tennis balls.

*You can e-mail them at www.bookwebpublishing.com

Answers on page 238.

Who are these humans?

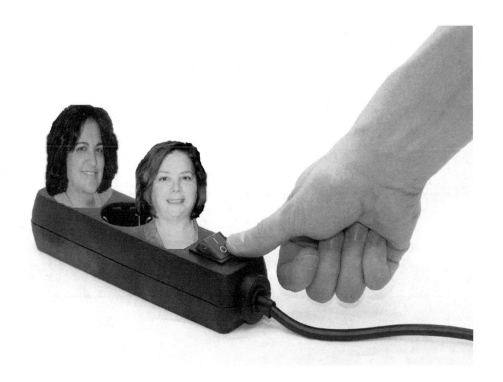

Clues

*They're best friends.

*They love kids.

*They love ice cream.

*They're very green.

*They write lots of books.

*They want humans to save energy.

Answers on page 238.

Who's Who?

Read each sentence then choose the right picture from the book. The answers are on page 238.

1. Who works at the power plant?

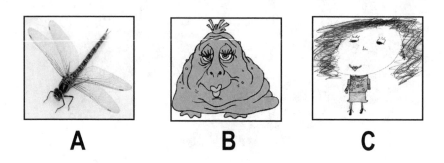

A   B   C

2. Who hates the people smell?

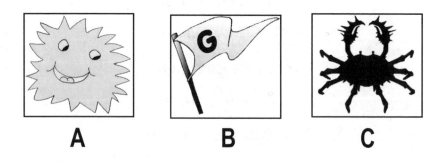

A   B   C

3. Who has the Amazing Tail Zap?

A   B   C

4. Who shows that garbage critters can be good?

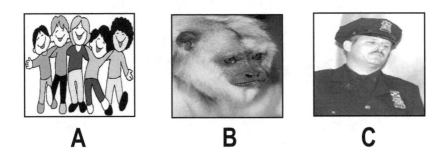

A   B   C

5. Who uses Meat Vision?

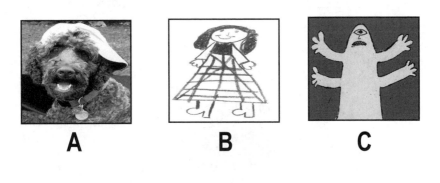

A   B   C

The Answers

page 234: Who are these critters?
The girl with the pointy hat is Coco; the guy with the sunglasses is The Giz. These Labradoodles were born in Rutland Manor, Australia. They spend a lot of time at school, motivating kids to read and write. They live in New York with author Jeri Fink and her husband Ricky.

page 235: Who are these humans?
They're authors Jeri Fink (at the end) and Donna Paltrowitz. They work with students to write books by kids for kids.

page 236-237:

1. B: Ms. Fossil Face

2. B: Dr. GreenWheels

3. A: Coco

4. C: Officer George

5. A: The Giz

Help the earth now.
Go green!

Coco and The Giz

Eco Notes

Eco Notes

Eco Notes

Eco Notes

Eco Notes

Eco Notes

Eco Notes